Baking

Spirits

Bright

Florence Gray

Cover and Illustrations by Kahns Design

Edited by Ioana Cheldiu

Printed in the United States of America

ISBN: 978-1-963836-92-9

For more about the author, visit: www.florencegray.org

10 9 8 7 6 5 4 3 2 1

A Letter to the Reader

Dear Reader,

First of all, thank you for choosing to spend part of your holiday season with this story. I hold this book especially close to my heart because Marjorie, Eliza's Nan, is inspired by someone very real to me: my own grandmother. She was warm, bubbly, bright, and full of life as ever, even until the end. Like Gretel's description of Mrs. Elle Toe, she was truly ruthless with a piping bag! (Though in my grandma's case, it extended to anything baking-related.)

At its core, this story is about found family, cherishing the loved ones we have, and finding joy in all of life's unexpected curveballs. Some readers may find Eliza frustrating in her hesitation to speak, or in her uneasiness when she does, but I wrote her with extreme intentionality. I see her as someone who has been deeply hurt and manipulated, someone who carries heavy insecurities and is slowly learning to navigate it. She finds steadiness and control best when she's working with her hands. She (usually) doesn't leap before she looks, except her stay at Gingerbread Hollow pushes her beyond what feels safe and familiar.

My hope is that her growth feels meaningful, profound, earned, and most importantly encouraging.

Merry Christmas!

xoxo,
Flor

*To my grandmother, for teaching me that
the sweetest things at any table
are love and kindness.*

"If I didn't know better, I'd think you were still around. What died didn't stay dead, you're alive in my head."
-Marjorie by Taylor Swift

Chapter One

Sticky Situations

Eliza Snow had survived a toxic ex, the most exhausting year of her life, and a winding mountain back road in the middle of a blizzard. At this point, she could endure anything.

Except for the inconvenient fact that a very real, very human man stood inside her fully paid for, fully solo Airbnb booking at Gingerbread Hollow.

The last thing she wanted was to be around people. But there it was: a cherry-red Land Rover half-buried in snow, parked outside her supposed little quiet getaway. Through the cabin's frosty window, she could make out the silhouette of a tall man standing inside the warm interior like the opening scene straight out of a Hallmark movie.

One she definitely hadn't auditioned for.

She stood there shivering in her pink, flour-speckled coat. One hand fumbled for the peppermint door handle of the cottage while the other wrestled her luggage over each of the gumdrop stepping stones as she tried to keep a sack of sugar tucked under her arm. The frigid winter air blew, sending her blonde hair plastering to her lip balm. She huffed, attempting an awkward shoulder-shimmy to shake the strands aside, but it was a lost cause. Her hands were too full, as it was—both literally and metaphorically.

The door opened, and she jumped backwards, nearly causing her to slip off the "Home Sweet Gingerbread Home" doormat. From inside, the smell of warm cinnamon and butter rolled out to greet her, carrying comforting memories of all her countless previous stays. It mingled with a newer, sharper note of evergreen that she couldn't quite place.

The sweet moment of nostalgia was cut short when she looked up and into a pair of honey-rich chocolate eyes. Eliza blinked, taken aback. First, by the fact that there was actually a stranger standing in her rental. Second, because the stranger was ridiculously attractive.

Everything about him was warm, starting with his eyes, which were hard not to stare into for their unique shade of hazel. Not hazel-green, but hazel-brown. His hair, a dark brunette, was textured in the most perfect kind of way, and his skin looked like he could've no sooner hopped off a plane from a month-long holiday in the Bahamas rather than the usual paleness that every other Brit sported this time of year.

She instantly regretted not dabbing on a bit of blush instead of climbing out of bed and heading straight here. Standing before him, she felt pale and washed out. Sallow, even. At the very least, she could've combed her hair, or maybe swept on a coat of mascara to make her blue eyes pop. Not that she cared what he thought of her eyes.

Davis had always preferred Eliza with perfectly lacquered nails and makeup. When she went without, he never said much positive—only remained silent that felt like judgment. He absolutely *loathed* her hair in a bun, especially when her highlights weren't fresh. That's when the comments came. How she was "*letting herself go*," or how he would oh-so-generously lend her some extra pounds for the salon, as if she couldn't handle it on her own.

Before him, she was never insecure about her appearance. Now, that's all she really ever was.

"Hi," she started, defaulting to the typical British politeness. "Excuse me, but what are you doing here?"

The man raised a brow, sipping hot chocolate from a "Let it Snow" mug. His sable hair looked like it'd been blown away from his angular face by the wind. He even had bits of ice still clinging to the tips of his hair, and his cheekbones were sharp enough to cut glass.

His eyes flicked to her suitcase and then her sack of sugar. He frowned, obviously as irritated to have company as she was. "I should be asking you that question, since this is my Airbnb," he answered flatly.

Eliza slowly blinked, her cheeks suddenly warm despite the bitter cold. "*Your* Airbnb?"

He took another sip of his cocoa, the chocolaty substance magically refilling itself with a gurgle. He extended his free hand. "The name's Lachlan Hollis. Booked this place through *SeasonalRetreats*. Confirmed. Paid. Non-refundable."

She gripped her suitcase, looking at his hand as if it were a slippery, raw chicken wing. Even if her hands weren't full, she wouldn't have shaken it. She'd had her fair share of the smug, contentious type.

Eliza was usually non-confrontational, but she narrowed her eyes into slits. If he only knew the year she'd had, he wouldn't be bold enough to test her. "That's not possible," she corrected. "I booked this place through *MagicalStays*. Also confirmed. Also non-refundable."

He just stood there in the warm air of the cottage and the growing awkwardness, even though he didn't look fazed in the slightest. The fire crackled in the hearth as if it were laughing at them, like they were two children fighting over the last biscuit. "There must be some mistake."

Propping her suitcase up on its wheels, she crossed her arms over her chest. "Is this not 2424 Drury Lane?"

"It is. I—" He finally seemed to notice her violently shivering. "You're cold. Come inside. We'll figure it out."

Seeing there was no other option, and the snow was up to the tires of her hire car she stepped inside, stamping off her boots by the threshold. The walls, floor, and ceiling were crusted with cinnamon, bits of the sugar glistening in the light. The windows were iced with delicate frosting, and the rafters of the vaulted ceiling above looked like a perfectly piped cake.

She stalked over to the hearth in the living room, outstretching her hands to warm them. The fireplace was on full blast, and the faint scorch marks on the rock candy mantle were just as she remembered them.

Everything about the cottage looked exactly as she remembered it, if not even more … *alive*.

She frowned when she saw the one exception to the rule, which was all of this Lachlan character's things. His duffel bags were piled high on the wingback chair, adjacent to the hearth. A thick wool blanket had already been pulled from the rack, and was draped over the sofa while a small retro TV played a Christmas movie in the background. He must've just been getting settled in for the night when she arrived.

She turned her back to the fire, allowing the warmth to seep into her backside as she assessed the rest of the cottage. In the kitchen sat a round table with bistro chairs, the window above the kitchen sink overlooked the small candy garden, and copper frypans hung from the ceiling over the island. Her eyes snagged on the baker's rack—cupboard fully stocked and filled to the brim with flour, vanilla, honey, and expensive ingredients Eliza hadn't seen since culinary school.

In this particular cottage, it seemed, every item magically restocked the moment it was used. The well of stock had no end. Her hands itched, eager to put that theory to the test as she did every season she came here.

For a moment, Lachlan and Eliza just stared at each other, unsure of what to say. The grandfather clock against the far wall *gonged* its amusement at the awkward exchange. Five o'clock.

She would've been elbows deep in dough by now if not for all this.

It was the week of Christmas. Couldn't anything go her way for once?

"Fine," Eliza muttered through gritted teeth. "I'll try contacting the rental company."

"Good." He ran his hands through his hair, looking relieved. "Maybe they can find another place you can stay for the holiday."

Eliza cut her eyes at him, throwing all pretense of friendliness right out the sugar-coated window. "Oh, *I'm* not the one leaving here."

"Well, I certainly don't want to leave. I was just starting to get settled. Plus, I got here first …" he muttered the last part, looking away from her and to the window.

Eliza's heart sputtered. "You don't get to call dibs on

the house just because you arrived first. I drove in from London, mind you. It was an absolute nightmare trying to book a rental at Saint Pancras Station, as you can imagine."

Lachlan smiled into his mug, now two-thirds of the way gone (and still magically refilling). "I guess we'll just have to avoid each other, then."

She placed a hand on her hip. "I don't want to *avoid you*. I paid for this rental, and I want to stay here. Alone."

He crossed his arms, not willing to budge. Seriously, did this man not grasp the meaning of generosity or sacrifice, especially during Christmas? "I drove five hours from Littlehampton through a blizzard, my phone signal went out completely, the road disappeared, and I went through a forest where trees literally threw snowballs at me. I'm not leaving," he declared.

A notification flashed across Eliza's screen. It was from the rental app. She clicked on it, eager to solve the mystery of the turn of events, but only a tiny circle swirled around and around for several long seconds.

"Great," she huffed. "The spinning wheel of death."

She waited several more seconds before clicking her screen off and shoving her mobile into her coat pocket. "I passed by the office when I pulled in." She marched to the door. "I'll just go back and have a chat with someone—"

She twisted the peppermint door handle. It didn't open. "*Seriously?*"

She pulled harder. The gingerbread rattled against the frame, but its sugary structure refused to budge. They were locked inside.

"Stupid house," she grumbled.

Her heart began to beat wildly in her chest. Was this how she was murdered? Had this man been stalking her, and now that she was alone in these enchanted woods, he finally had the chance?

Maybe she watched too much true crime, but she refused to be another psychopath's victim.

Lachlan came up behind her, and she instantly regretted not grabbing a butter knufe from the drawer. He tugged on the door.

"Careful," he pointed upwards toward the house, casually crossing the kitchen back to his steaming cup of cocoa. He took another sip, resting against the island as if it was just another average Tuesday for him. "It can hear you, you know."

She whipped around, stalking toward the kitchen window. If she had to, she wasn't afraid of busting out of a sugar-blown window to make her escape. "Yes, I know it can hear me. I've been here plenty of times—"

Her mouth dropped open when she tossed the sugar-laced curtain aside.

"Um … Lachlan?" She tested his name on her lips, hoping she pronounced it right. She'd never heard the name before, and if she'd been less distracted by the sudden blizzard outside, or trying to discern if he was a threat or not, she might've been inclined to think how fond of the name she was.

Lachlan crossed the room in two long strides, coming over to stand next to her to peer out the window. The world beyond them had vanished into white. Snow wasn't just falling—it *poured* from the sky, like confectioners' sugar being sifted through a massive grate. The flurries blanketed everything in sight.

She realized then that it wasn't the house that smelled of evergreen. It wasn't even a Christmas tree, because, as her eyes quickly swept over the place, she found not a single twinkling light or a pine needle in sight.

It was Lachlan, and the bite of something warmer underneath, like a cinnamon ornament tucked into delicate branches.

He whistled. "Better make yourself comfortable. Looks like neither of us is going anywhere for a while."

Her hands were shaky, uneasy with his sudden closeness, as she pulled out her phone again and quickly typed out a message to her friend, Piper.

> White sweater. Ripped high-waisted jeans. Pale pink coat. That was the last thing I wore in case I go missing.

She waited for the *shoomp* of the message to tell her it went through, but the text bubble turned green instead. She cursed under her breath.

Lachlan lifted his hands, as if noticing that she felt

like she was backed into a corner. Which she was. "Look—I'll take the couch. There's a single bedroom upstairs that you can stay in. It locks. Just need to get my clothes out of it."

"Flipping heck," Eliza muttered, her body still humming from her earlier panic. "The rest of my luggage is in my car. I don't have any other clothes."

And seeing as neither of them could go outside without getting blown away by the snow—assuming they could even get the door open.

Why hadn't she just put on something a bit more comfortable for the journey here? Of course, she hadn't expected the enchanted house to lock her inside before she could grab any of her things.

Back when Eliza was a girl, she hadn't ever recalled the cottage being magically faulty or the weather ever being this extreme. It was a weird year, all around.

Lachlan blew out a breath, running a hand through his hair. "Just borrow whatever you need from me. It's just one night."

"Are you sure?" she asked, brow raised. "I'll get powdered sugar on one of your fancy flannels."

"So will I." Lachlan shrugged. "We're literally in a gingerbread house," he pointed out.

She cracked a faint smile. "Fair point. But just so you know, I'll be baking and pretending like you don't exist."

She was thankful for the gesture so she could, at the very least, get out of these jeans and into some sweatpants. But that didn't mean she had to converse with him.

"Deal." He casually leaned against the island, kicking his feet out. His socks had elves wearing ugly Christmas sweaters on them. "You can wear my clothes in exchange for a pastry."

"It sounds like you get the sweeter deal," Eliza shot him a glare.

"You're in no position to bargain. Unless you'd like to stay in jeans all night long."

She narrowed her eyes. "Are you blackmailing me?"

"The way I see it, I'd call it Negotiation," he said. "I'm an estate agent, so I come by it honestly."

"Estate agent, huh? Planning to move into your forever home here on Drury Lane?"

His laugh lacked amusement. "No. Actually, my sister sent me here as an early Christmas present. She said I needed to 'get away.'"

Eliza thought for a moment. "Did your sister make the reservation? Maybe she forgot to complete some form online, and that's why you're here—"

"My sister's an orthopedic surgeon," he cut in. "I think she knows how to use a bloody booking app."

He blew out a breath as he looked out the window again. He looked wishful that all the snow might magically melt so that this impromptu snow-in party could come to an end. She followed his gaze, hopeful too. But the snow was falling at a sharp forty-five degree angle.

There was no escaping this mess anytime soon.

Bang! Something slammed against the back door. Eliza jumped. Lachlan grabbed the handle and swung it open. Before she could question how he managed to get the door open this time, a gust of sparkling flurries came pillaging in. Beyond it was a solid wall of ice. The snow outside pulsed, glowing bright orange.

Then, bursting through the snow and into the kitchen came a tiny gingerbread dragon, flaming at the mouth.

Chapter Two

Enchanted Gingersnaps

The gingerbread dragon shot from one end of the kitchen to the other in a festive sweet-smelling frenzy. It couldn't have been any bigger than a kitten, with bulging lavender eyes the size of gumdrops. Its wings were decorated with pink and green icing. The sugar encrusting them left a trail of dust in its wake as it flapped around madly, doing circles from the kitchen to the living room.

Eliza gawked, not believing her eyes. "Wonderful. There's a miniature biscuit lizard in my kitchen."

The creature barreled into the baker's rack, knocking

a jar of white chocolate chips off the shelf. As soon as the jar of sugar-glass shattered and a thousand tiny candies scattered, the jar reappeared, magically restored with more chocolate chips inside. Eliza blinked, doubly shocked.

It had been years since she'd witnessed the magic of this cottage—she'd seen it plenty of times before when she came here with her nan—but that didn't make it any less jarring. Still, she'd never seen a flying hatchling of any kind before.

Lachlan, however, seemed immediately taken with the creature, as if it was an everyday occurrence that a living, breathing gingerbread dragon came flying into his life.

"Hey little bloke," Lachlan greeted with a smile.

Eliza couldn't help noticing how gently Lachlan approached the creature. Slow, careful, and leaving it room to breathe. Not out of fear, but out of respect for its personal space. And the irony wasn't lost on her, considering she was stuck with him for the evening, forced to share the gingerbread house.

Lachlan looked up from where he was bent over, flashing Eliza an apologetic smile. "I kind of have a thing for strays."

Eliza gave something like a "hmph," displeased with the turn of events. She crossed her arms. It wasn't that she didn't like animals. She loved them, actually. She'd always wanted a cat, but her fiancé—*ex*-fiancé—had been allergic.

She just didn't want the extra stress. Not this week. Maybe that meant she was a little selfish, or maybe it just meant she was exhausted.

Still, Eliza's fingers twitched, eager to reach out and get to work, but Lachlan and the frosting fire hazard were both still present.

Sensing her dissatisfaction, Lachlan quirked up a brow. "I take it you don't like animals, then?"

"Animals? No, I actually quite like them. Sentient flying sugar biscuits? I haven't decided yet." She eyed the creature, who was now sniffing about the place like a dog on a mission to find its missing treat. "Though, I will say you both have lost points in your favor for keeping me from what I came here to do."

"Oh, yeah?" Lachlan straightened, eyes running over her blonde hair, fresh manicure, and pale pink cable-knit jumper. "What'd I do, ruin your weekend retreat with your book club?"

"What? Absolutely not," she sputtered.

"Emergency mad shopping trip for more pastel winter jumpers?"

She let out a huff, not amused in the slightest by his teasing. "Look, can we not just put him back outside?" Eliza protested. "He can clearly heat himself up, it's not like he'll get frostbite."

In answer, the dragon narrowed its glowing eyes at her. A sound somewhere between a hiss and a sizzle came from the back of its throat.

Point taken.

Lachlan settled himself onto a vanilla wafer barstool. "He might be hungry. Maybe he'll like the pastries you're going to make for us."

"For *me*," Eliza corrected, already digging through her mental go-to of holiday recipes. "The pastries *I'm* going to make for *me*. If you're lucky, you can have one single pastry."

What did a gingerbread dragon eat, anyways?

"One pastry per clothing article," Lachlan bargained, holding up a finger in objection.

Before Eliza could argue, the dragon fluttered over to her, sniffing at the icing crusted in her hair. She stood perfectly still, worried that one wrong move might cause her to go up in flames. Instead, it nuzzled the side of its jaw into Eliza's shoulder, like a cat grazing against its owner's leg.

"Okay, that's adorable," Lachlan said, and Eliza couldn't say she disagreed.

The dragon, sensing he was being observed, fluttered over to Lachlan next. Eliza could've sworn she saw the dragon's tail wagging.

Lachlan laughed, reaching out to boop the gingerbread dragon on the nose. The dragon blew a puff of smoke at him and rumbled a low growl in warning.

"Careful," Eliza said over her shoulder. "Looks like you might be his next victim."

"Guess that explains the scorch marks on the wall," Lachlan muttered. "What should we call him?"

Eliza raised her brows. "Call him? We're not keeping him."

Lachlan and the sentient pastry both shot her a look.

"Fine." Eliza rolled her eyes, not willing to put up a fight. She couldn't say she was happy about it. Not in the slightest. Not only would she now be in the company of a complete stranger for the evening, but she now had a pet to take care of.

Despite her temptation, she knew she couldn't kick either of them out in the middle of a snowstorm. "Keep things ticking over while I go upstairs. Do you mind if I borrow those clothes now?" She was already tired of wearing jeans.

Lachlan nodded politely, crossing the room and pulling out a festive t-shirt and a pair of gray sweats. He offered the clothes to her with an eyebrow raised, "Hope you like Christmas shirts. That's all I packed this week."

Eliza took the clothes without looking and headed up the stairs, murmuring her thanks.

The bedroom was as she remembered. Quaint and cozy. She stalked over to the bedside table, and in its drawer, she found the guest-book log. She parted the leatherbound book, one of very few things in the house that wasn't edible, and scanned over the names until she found her nan's curly handwriting.

Marjorie Elizabeth Snow

Tears gathered as she traced her finger over every lacy letter of the signature her nan once used on every Christmas gift tag, and at the bottom of her grocery lists. Not here, though. Here, the baking supplies never ran short.

She pulled out her mobile and snapped a picture of it before shutting the guest-list book and setting it back on the nightstand. In the bathroom, the sugar-spun tile was the same outdated geometric-green pattern. As a kid, she used to run her finger along the edges of the design for what felt like hours until she went cross-eyed. And there, on the door, her tiny, smeared handprint was still there from the time she finger-painted and got a little too excited that she forgot to stay on the paper.

Her nan scrubbed and scrubbed until Eliza was certain the wall would've crumbled underneath Nan's forceful grip, but the damage was done. It was forever a part of the house—just like the memory of her nan was forever branded into the very presence of it.

So many fond memories. So many good holidays spent here.

Eliza shrugged out of her sweater and into Lachlan's t-shirt. She couldn't help but note the sharp evergreen scent, which seemed to surround her now in a relentless cloud. She couldn't help herself as she breathed it in repeatedly, enjoying the fragrance. He smelled of peppermints and Christmas trees, with a blend of a manly sort of musk that Eliza couldn't place.

She glanced in the mirror and rolled her eyes. It was a band t-shirt with the graphic of a hand in the "Rock and Roll" symbol, and the slogan above saying: "Sleighing It."

Whatever. She wasn't going to a fashion show. And she certainly wouldn't feel insecure in these baggy clothes. She was here for one reason, and one alone. It wasn't to look cute or impress anyone. She did, however, pinch her cheeks and nose, cursing the storm outside for not allowing her to get into her makeup bag.

She stalked back down the stairs and rounded the corner to find Lachlan sitting at the kitchen island, hanging a treat over the dragon's nose, commanding the creature to sit.

The dragon was wagging its tail with its head cocked to one side, but it wasn't listening.

Lachlan glanced over at Eliza. "He doesn't know how to sit."

"Or he does, and he's choosing to ignore you." She leaned against the counter.

She swore she saw the little dragon cast her a wink. "So. Back to naming you." She eyed the dragon.

He eyed her back.

Eliza thought for a minute. "How about Biscuit?"

The little dragon pastry audaciously made a gagging noise before flapping over to the baker's rack, this time much more carefully than before. With a delicate wing, he tapped on a little metal tin of recipe cards, making sure not to topple anything else over in the process.

"Not Biscuit, I take it?" Eliza giggled, opening the box for him. He shook his head back and forth vigorously, extending his wing even further. "What is it you want in here?"

She sifted through each colorful cardstock page one by one, each recipe more enticing than the next. *Yuletide Christmas Cake, North Pole Panettone, Pistachio and White Chocolate Stollen, and Jingle Bell Bundt Cake ...*

The collection was massive, and the possibilities swirled in her mind as she tried to narrow down which sweet treat she would craft first. Some of the recipes even sparkled faintly, as if competing for her attention.

Her fingers thrummed across one labeled "*Reindeer Chow.*" Before she could pull it free, a low growling noise rumbled through the dragon. His gumdrop eyes narrowed at the recipe card, hissing his displeasure.

"Not a fan of reindeer chow?" Eliza asked. To her amazement, the little fire-breathing biscuit shook his head. He batted his wings, planted his feet on the rim of the tin box and shuffled through each card with his snout.

Eliza couldn't help but smile. "You've got opinions now, huh?"

He stopped once he reached a card labeled "*Gingerbread Snap Dragons.*"

Eliza's mouth dropped open. This was the recipe card that made him. And he wanted to *eat* them? "You can't be serious. You want me to make these?"

Now that she knew he could understand what she was saying, she certainly wasn't going to voice that she didn't wish to make any more pastries of his kind.

The dragon shook his head again, nudging her with his gumdrop and pointing at the name. "Oh, I see," retorted Eliza. "You're trying to tell me what you are!"

The dragon nodded his head yes in response.

"But that isn't your actual name, is it?" She blinked.

Another shake.

"Well, what is it, then?" she asked.

With his snout, he began shifting through the cards again until he stopped. He tapped a word halfway down the page.

"*Puffcake ...*" she recited. Her eyes shot wide. "That's your name. Your name is Puffcake!"

The creature flapped his wings, barking as he spun midair.

A genuine laugh escaped Eliza's lips, one of the first since the breakup and the shop closing down. "Well, Puffcake, I think it's only fitting that we first paid homage to your name. Do you mind grabbing two eggs from the fridge?"

She'd never made Puffcake, and, truth be told, she wasn't exactly sure what they were. She was just excited to get stuck with anything that involved baking.

"Call me if you need a taste tester," Lachlan said. "I'll be here reading about the rising interest rates, if anyone needs me." He gathered his laptop from the counter and headed toward the living room.

"Sounds great," Eliza gave a little sing-song as she rinsed her hands at the sink. "But just so you know, I won't need you."

Finally, she thought. *Finally, I get to bake alone. Or at least, almost alone.*

The cabinet door flew open and slammed into Lachlan's kneecap. A *crack* sounded, and he grumbled under his breath, trying not to curse from the impact.

Puffcake and Eliza exchanged a glance. "A-are you okay?" Eliza asked, shocked.

"Never better." Lachlan turned around, jaw set tightly.

"I swear neither of us did that." Eliza held her hands up in innocence. Puffcake followed suit, but let out a little snort.

Lachlan narrowed his eyes at Puffcake, but said nothing, only slowly turning around again to cross the threshold into the living room. Again, he was met with the cabinet doors stopping him from exiting.

He ran a hand through his hair. "I think it's giving me a cheeky 'not-so-fast.'"

Eliza's shoulders slumped. She looked about the house like it had eyes and could see her displeasure. "Can you try again? This time, just try walking really slowly so the door doesn't hit you hard."

Lachlan tried a third time. The cabinet seemed to swing open harder than before, knocking into his other knee. "Ow!" he howled, and Eliza cupped her hand to her mouth.

"Sorry." She winced. "I feel like that was my fault."

"No worries." Lachlan waved her off. "I'm just going to sit right here, if that's okay." Lachlan half-walked, half-limped over to the island and took a seat again. He opened his laptop—or at least tried to—but the top wouldn't unlatch from the bottom. It was like the laptop had been glued shut.

They all stared down at it, amazed. Lachlan raised an eyebrow at Eliza. "Is this some sort of cruel joke to get me to leave?"

"What?" Eliza choked out. "You think I'm behind all this?"

He just shrugged, leaning back in the chair and crossing his arms.

"I was halfway across the room when the cabinet went berserk. And I'm not cruel enough to glue your laptop closed." When Lachlan still didn't look convinced, Eliza placed a hand on her hip. "Look, I didn't want to share this cottage with anyone this week. Why would I purposefully try and keep you in the same room as me?"

He didn't answer immediately. Eliza raised her brows at him, expectant.

They locked eyes, neither of them willing to back down as the grandfather clock marked every painful, heavy second. The house seemed to chuckle its delight at the cruel little irony of the scene.

Lachlan finally raised his hands in surrender. "By all means, don't let me, or the house, try and keep you from your baking."

"Fine," Eliza said, lips tight. "But *don't* expect me to keep you company. Soon, I'll be in my zone, and I won't want to chit-chat with you about interest rates or fancy beach houses. Got it?"

Lachlan gave a silent salute. In response, the kitchen began pulling ingredients from the recipe card. Eliza never had to lift a finger and instead just watched the magic of the cottage unfold around her.

Chapter Three

Burnt Bread

E liza sighed contentedly to herself, tying off the mint green apron around her waist. Already, the butter was softening on the counter, the cupboard doors splaying open to reveal more baking goods with hand-written labels.

Puffcake turned out to be the perfect companion to be snowed in with. Unlike Lachlan, Puffcake hardly took up any space; he didn't mind if Eliza retreated into the safety of her own thoughts, and, best of all, he didn't speak.

"So ..." Lachlan sighed. "Do you have any family back home?"

Eliza didn't answer. She tried to ignore the feeling that she was being closely watched as she pulled back her long hair into a loose topknot before setting off to work. She searched for a lighter in every crust-filled drawer, to no avail. Then she got an idea.

"Puffcake?" she called out. "Do you mind blowing fire onto the cooker while I turn the gas on?"

Happy to be of use, he did as she requested. She turned the knob on the hob, the fire-starter clicking in protest. Puffcake blew a line of fire onto the cooker, and the gentle flames erupted in a low purr.

"A sister? Cousin?" Lachlan tried again. "Once or twice removed?"

It'd been *five minutes* since she'd laid down the groundwork about how this evening would go, and he still was asking questions.

Eliza turned to him and gave a slow, frustrated blink. "I thought I said no chatting."

"Technically, you laid strict guidelines that I was not to speak about my job, mostly. Not that I couldn't ask questions about your personal life," Lachlan ever-so-kindly pointed out.

Eliza massaged her temples. "Okay. New rule. No chatting about *anything*. Not just interest rates and beach houses."

Lachlan blew out a breath into his mug of hot chocolate. "C'mon, mate, that's not fair. What am I supposed to do besides just sit here and drink hot choco-late? You at least have your baking to keep you busy.

My laptop still refuses to open." He frowned at the device.

"I don't know," Eliza gave a fake smile. "With all due respect, that isn't my problem."

"Could I offer you a helping hand?"

"No, thank you," she sing-songed politely as she continued to stir the batter.

"I'm practically a chocolatier expert after watching seven seasons of the Great British Bake Off" he bragged.

"Not making chocolate," she stirred more forcefully, "but still, no."

Lachlan decided to give up, just picked up the recipe tin, and began going through the recipe cards one by one. He read them off, muttering to himself how he'd like to bake this one, or how he'd never have the patience to complete that one.

Somehow, Eliza tuned him out as best she could, receding into her own thoughts as she cracked the egg, creamed the butter, and churned in the molasses. Puff-cake made an excellent assistant, wordlessly reaching for the ingredients and already having them measured for Eliza so she wouldn't have to concern herself with the exact proportions.

It was nice to have a helping hand in the kitchen, both from Puffcake and from the enchanted kitchen. It strangely reminded her of the days she'd spent her Christmases here as a child with her nan, learning how to bake in this very space. Though she hadn't remembered ever seeing Puffcake before, or any creature quite like him.

She did remember, however, the magic. The art. The skill. She remembered watching her grandmother's bony hands as they rolled dough, stirred batter, and poured caramel drizzle over the freshly made cake. She remembered the laughs that reverberated through the cottage walls late into the evening as the two of them talked and tasted to their hearts' content.

She hadn't realized it then, but her grandmother's company had been the magic all along.

A smile spread across Eliza's lips at the sweet memory of her. When she baked, she always felt like she wasn't so far away anymore.

The thought suddenly turned bitter as she remembered why she was back here to begin with. It wasn't for the holiday, but to escape.

Back in London, she'd felt like the dough she placed in the oven every morning: expected to rise and perform even though she'd been stretched too thin. Owning her own business had been hard enough, but partnering with someone who couldn't fully commit? Impossible.

Davis couldn't commit to the bakery, or to her.

Sometimes she regretted giving it up. The license, the name, the menu, and even the cute little brick and mortar building the color of a robin's egg. Every day, she missed it. Every day, she wondered if she had made the right decision to leave.

But she'd been cornered. And Davis always knew how to win a fight.

Now, she worked for a corner café serving flapjacks, mushy peas, and coffee to a loyal stream of old, dying, and grumbling population. The owners were good to her; steady, salt-of-the-earth kind of people, but she missed the freedom. The *creativity*. The serene yet hustle and bustle of making something entirely her own.

Only, if she ever were to have another opportunity to do something like that again, she'd do so much differently. She'd do it right.

Eliza glanced at the clock, the hour hand pointing to eight in the evening. How did she seem to always enter a time warp when she started baking?

"I've never had a puffcake," Lachlan stated. "What about you, Puffcake?"

Puffcake shook his head before twisting back around to help Eliza finish off preparing the last batch of the desserts. Seemed like he'd even grown tired of conversation.

Lachlan sighed heavily, scooting away from his seat. He slowly inched his way over toward where Eliza was working, as if waiting for permission to come closer. She didn't give it.

"Behind," he muttered, taking a pan from the counter and waving it neatly over her head.

"What are you doing?" she asked.

"I'm going to cook dinner. I'll need more than just butter and sugar to fill me up." As if on cue, his stomach rumbled. He snagged another apron from the hook and tied it around his waist. Eliza couldn't help but snicker. It was pink with jolly looking Santas printed all over.

They worked around each other in tandem, darting between counters and cupboards. Each reached for spoons, bowls, and spices, and the kitchen seemed to hum along to their rhythm, opening drawers as they needed, or sliding them closed when they were done. At one point, their synchronized pattern faltered, and their hands both grabbed the salt at the same time.

Eliza jerked hers back as if the jar had scorched her.

Flour canisters drifted closer, Puffcake fluttered around doing preliminary taste-tests, and the oven door swung open wide no sooner than when the timer dinged. She placed the steaming puffcakes down on the counter, leaving them to cool.

"They're done!" Eliza piped up, placing the plate of puffcakes in the center of the island.

They each took a bite, and the warm icing melted on Eliza's tongue, the orange and nutmeg notes blending in the most perfect harmony. She couldn't help but moan her delight as she took another bite, thoroughly pleased with herself. She'd followed the rules on the recipe card just enough to honor the recipe, and broken other rules where it counted.

Lachlan stole a glance at her, and a blush settled on her cheeks. "Sorry," she washed the remnants of the first cake down with a glass of milk. He laughed, looking at

Puffcake next, who was vigorously lapping up his third pastry like a dog.

"Well, how do you like them?" she asked Lachlan eagerly. If she was going to share his company until this weather blew over, he would at least need to enjoy her baking.

"Oh, they're splendid—uh …" he gulped, looking down at his plate. "You know, I just realized that you never gave me your name."

"Eliza," she said. "Eliza Snow."

"So, Lachlan Hollis gets snowed in with Eliza Snow." A slow smile spread across his face, softening the edges of his features. He was handsome. The kind of handsome that snuck up on you when he wasn't busy being smug, or ruining week-long solo trips.

"Don't forget Puffcake," she added.

"Right. How could I ever forget?"

"Help yourself to at least one more puffcake," she said. "I'll need another t-shirt to sleep in tonight, if that's okay."

Her apron, and somehow, her clothes underneath, were both speckled with sugar. She was always a messy baker, a habit from childhood that even her nan couldn't break.

Puffcake reclined backwards on the windowsill and blew out a breath of powdered sugar. Clearly, he wasn't hungry anymore.

"Don't get me wrong, the puffcakes are great,"

Lachlan rose from his seat, licking the icing from his fingers. "But I was preparing a salad to go with the pizza I'm about to put in the oven."

Eliza snorted. "Good luck finding anything else in this kitchen other than baking supplies." Lachlan opened the freezer and pulled out a grocery bag with a frozen pepperoni pizza. She snarled at the sight. "Don't tell me you brought that here."

"I brought survival food. And it's a good thing I did because we'd be absolutely famished." His eyes cut to the window and the blizzard beyond it, to prove his point.

"What you call an emergency, I call a proper dog's breakfast."

"C'mon, Snow." He smiled, already reaching for a pan. "We're in the middle of a snowstorm. Now's not the time for refined dining. And it's not like we can pop by any of the restaurants here."

She wrinkled her nose. "Still. Even during desperate times, I have standards."

"Well, good for you. Suppose you've earned a biscuit for all your poshness." He slid the ready meal into the oven and set a timer on his mobile.

A thunderous *bang* rattled the biscuit jars on the countertop. Smoke billowed from the oven, and the house filled with the distinct scent of charred food.

Lachlan stared. Eliza smugly crossed her arms over her chest. "Guess the house has standards, too."

The oven door clattered open and spat the burnt pizza out across the kitchen. Lachlan ran his hands through his hair, defeated. "Fine," he breathed out. "Another puffcake it is, then."

Chapter Four

Baking at Midnight

Eliza stood at the kitchen counter cradling the tin full of recipes. The metal was cool beneath her touch, and the lid squeaked as she opened it. She grazed over each of the hand-written cards, each page smudged with butter stains. A small thrill coursed through her, excited to lose herself in another baking project.

Her fingers lingered over each of the edges, waiting for one recipe to call to her rather than the other way around.

Over in the living room came the faint sound of Lachlan's breathing. He was fast asleep on the couch with one hand covering his eyes, his chest rising and falling softly. Beneath the kitchen's windowsill, Puff-cake claimed a small mixing bowl as his bed, snoring loudly in a sugar-induced coma. Puffs of smoke billowed from his nostrils.

Then the house stirred. A loud, sudden *thump* disrupted the quiet, causing Eliza to jump. A book had fallen from the baker's rack behind her, the spine hitting the floor with a solid crack. Eliza bent to pick it up, smoothing her palm over the worn cover the color of absinthe.

She swore the gold title glimmered underneath her fingers: *Isadora's Memory Baking Cookbook*.

Eliza hesitated momentarily before opening it. Her heart thrummed in her chest as she thumbed through the brittle pages with care. Each word on the page floated to life, as if revealing the truest nature of the book to her.

Some of the instructions seemed odd. It was more than just ingredients and baking times. It included things like "*Stir counterclockwise thrice on a new moon*" and "*Sing a Christmas carol to encourage the dough to rise.*"

She sucked in a breath. These weren't just recipes. They were *spells*. But it wasn't the only odd thing about this book. Written on the very front page in delicate penmanship was a rhyme:

This cookbook belongs to Isadora Black.
Always remember to start at the first,
and bake 'til the last.
Skip not a single step, nor bake too fast.

Eliza read off the first recipe. She couldn't explain it, but it felt warm and inviting, like it almost *wanted* to be picked. In a way, it felt less like Eliza was sifting through recipes and more like she was peeking into someone's personal diary. In her own family, recipes were sacred, passed down like heirlooms and kept close like secrets.

Baking at Midnight: Memory Making Meringue (Only to be baked at the stroke of twelve.)

She glanced at the grandfather clock. Five minutes to spare.

She was so eager to gather the ingredients that her fingers tapped on the cookbook nervously, but a moment of hesitation seized her. Was Eliza *allowed* to use this cookbook?

Surely so, or else it wouldn't have almost literally fallen into her hands. Right? Besides, the house had a way of expressing its feelings. If it didn't want her using these recipes, she knew it would stop her. It could've hidden the instructions in blotted ink stains and smudges, or not have revealed the recipes at all.

Quickly getting to work, she rounded up the ingredients from the shelf and mixed in a hurry. Unlike most times, she followed this recipe to the letter, every stir and measure.

She stirred with vigor and felt an odd sense of warmth blooming over her. Vanilla and lemon zest filled the air in a cloud of festive cheer, and, just as she cracked the last egg, the batter shimmered.

The grandfather clock struck twelve as soon as Eliza placed the pan inside the oven.

Now she knew why the recipe insisted it be baked at midnight. The instructions demanded it, down to the minute. The meringue wouldn't bake a moment before or after.

While she waited, she thought to flip through more of the recipes in the book, studying each of the desserts that gave her a mysterious inclination to bake them.

In all her times she'd come to visit, she never remembered seeing this cookbook before. She wondered if it even *was* here the last time or if there was a reason it jumped out at her now. Or had it falling from the shelf merely been a coincidence?

But it was placed far enough away from the edge of the baker's rack for it not to be chalked up to an accident …

She half-expected at any moment for the oven to spit out the meringues as it had the pizza earlier that evening. But ten minutes later, she was taking the meringues from the oven and setting them down to cool on the countertop. Once they were at room temperature, she popped one of the puffs into her mouth. Buttery, crunchy goodness flooded her senses, and her heart swelled once more with fulfillment.

Then, the kitchen around her shifted.

Sleeping Puffcake was nowhere in sight, the glow of the crescent moon was creeping through the curtains, and the counters were spotless. A stark difference to the organized chaos they had been just moments before.

Eliza wiped at her eyes, positive she must be hallucinating. And, for all practical purposes, Eliza *was* hallucinating.

A young woman glided through, moving like the winter chill couldn't touch her. She wore an apron the color of sunshine, and her smile lit up the room, equally as bright. Her cheeks were dusted with blush and flour as she fluttered about the kitchen, whisking something inside a copper bowl.

Behind her, a young man with short hair the color of butter approached, wrapping his arms around her as he showered her in a series of kisses. She giggled, playfully swatting him away. He then popped a familiar-looking dollop of meringue into his mouth.

"Isadora," he dramatically sighed, his Irish accent thicker than molasses. "You are absolute magic."

The woman, Isadora, turned her attention away from the counter and gazed up into the man's hazel eyes. She looked at him with such happiness and contentment that it made Eliza's chest tighten. Isadora patted his cheek playfully. "Good thing you married a witch. Magic's as common as flour around here."

He brushed an onyx strand of hair away from the young woman's porcelain face and pulled her in close. Eliza's cheeks heated at the lovers' embrace. She suddenly felt like she was intruding, but couldn't look away. She, too, once had someone look at her the way this man looked at Isadora.

"There is nothing common about you, sweet girl," the man whispered in the crux of her neck.

Isadora arched into his touch, giggling softly. "I love you, Ernest."

"I love you, too." He smiled back at her, brightly. "Earnestly."

The young man bent low to kiss her just as the grandfather clock gonged twelve times. Then the lovely scene in front of her was gone.

She was standing in the same spot she'd been in before she was transported away through the vision. Only, she hadn't seen a vision.

It had been a *memory*.

Isadora's Memory *Baking Cookbook*. Of course. Isadora Black was the owner, and, through the recipes, she was showing memories of her life, ones that had taken place here in this very cottage.

But what Eliza still couldn't quite make out was this: Who was this Isadora Black, and why was she showing Eliza memories of her past?

Chapter Five

Eggnog and Wi-Fi

For breakfast, Eliza prepared coffee and honey butter buns with eggs on the side. The eggs were the exception on her very short list of items she could actually cook—and most of them were breakfast-related dishes.

She stood in the kitchen, dressed in Lachlan's sweatpants and a t-shirt sporting a gingerbread man with a crumbled leg, the caption *"Oh Snap,"* written on it. She'd changed into it shortly before she retired to bed late in the morning. Puffcake hadn't liked the concept of the new t-shirt one bit. He took one look at it when she came down the stairs and had been throwing looks of disapproval in Eliza's direction ever since.

"Hey, don't judge me." She threw her hands up when she entered the room. "This is Lachlan's t-shirt, not mine."

That seemed to appease Puffcake for the time being, because he fluttered over to Eliza's side and perched militantly on her shoulder, like a lion surveying his pride.

His flight was significantly slower than it had been yesterday, and with red crumbs that dotted his face, it was the only tell that she'd made red velvet biscuits last night. The rest of the biscuits were "mysteriously" gone from the cloche she'd placed them under.

The biscuits had been the second recipe of Isadora's cookbook, and with it came another vision, just as it had the first time. As soon as Eliza took a bite of the freshly baked dessert, she was dropped into the witch's romantic world once more.

It had been only moments after the first memory took place. Isadora had said something to tease her beau, Ernest, before swiping her finger in the crimson batter and bopping him on the nose.

He kissed her all over, smearing the batter on her neck, chest, and rosy cheeks before scooping her up and stomping them both up the stairs. Eliza didn't follow, but heard their shouts of playful giggles all the way up until the door slammed shut behind them.

Lachlan came around the corner, and Puffcake

snubbed up his nose. Lachlan wrinkled his brows, confused by Puffcake's coldness until he glanced Eliza's way. After noting the shirt, he just laughed. "Looks like I'll be getting the cold shoulder the rest of the day."

"In his defense, you did pack a graphically offensive T-shirt," Eliza pointed out. She smiled as she rubbed the dragon's underbelly, and he kicked his foot repeatedly in satisfaction.

"We're going to have to start giving you rations, Puffcake. I'm not even sure where you store all of that cake you ate," added Eliza. Or how it was possible for him to eat in the first place, or how he was sentient … There was a lot about Puffcake that she didn't quite understand. Or about this cottage, apparently.

But a thought crossed her mind.

"Puffcake," she paused her scratching to ask him a serious question. "Did anything strange happen to you after you ate the red velvet biscuits last night?"

Puffcake yawned, innocently shaking his head. He wasn't even suspicious of her questioning in the slightest.

Interesting. If the magic didn't work on him, how was *she* able to see it?

Lachlan wandered sleepily into the kitchen. "Good morning, by the way," he yawned, coming over to the coffee pot to fill his cup. He parted the curtain above the kitchen sink as he took a swig.

The snow was still falling, but not as aggressively as it had the night before. The gingerbread cottage was so covered in it that it looked like a child had gone a little too crazy with extra icing.

She placed two plates down on the round table and a significantly smaller plate down on the windowsill for Puffcake.

Eliza couldn't help but be grateful for the silence as they ate. Lachlan had thanked her for making breakfast and even complimented her on the eggs. Though she didn't know how to take it.

She knew they were a far cry from her baking, but she made them enough at the diner back home to know how to prepare them right.

Maybe he was just being nice. Or maybe he meant it?

She suddenly felt a prick of guilt for how cold she'd treated him yesterday. "I'm sorry. For yesterday." She bit out the words. "I know all this isn't exactly ideal for either of us, but I should've been a little nicer about it." She stuck her hand out for him to shake, calling for a truce.

His large hand wrapped around hers, and she couldn't help but notice how warm and how much larger it was than her own. "Don't worry about it," he smiled. "I'll be honest, I was a little bummed, too. But I'll keep you around for the time being if you promise to continue baking."

Once he finished his plate, he scooted away from the table, finished off the last of his coffee, and headed for the door. He pulled on his boots and shrugged on his thick winter coat.

"Where are you going?" Eliza asked.

"To shovel the driveway. That way, you can, at the very least, get out if you need to. Or go for a walk."

Eliza's cheeks bloomed as she looked down at her unfinished plate of food. *She* wasn't leaving. Why did he just assume that she would be the one to do so? It was a thoughtful gesture, but she wondered how much of it was for her and how much of it was to bribe her to leave.

This was her cottage, the one she always returned to every Christmas. And now, she felt like she had a mystery to solve, a puzzle to keep her mind occupied. Her eyes flitted to Isadora's Cookbook, longing to try the next dessert.

Eliza thought it prudent not to share her late-night baking escapade with Lachlan.

She had to be careful. She couldn't make the recipes during the day while Lachlan was awake, in case he saw the desserts and wanted to taste them. She wasn't sure if the memory hadn't worked on Puffcake because he wasn't human, or if they only worked for her, but she didn't want to find out.

She would have to wait until he was asleep. Until then, she would bake some more of her own creations.

Puffcake helped her fire up the cooker just as Lachlan, once again getting the hint she wasn't in for conversation, set for the door. The lock was still jammed.

"Great," he said, throwing up his hands. "We're going to die here."

"A bit dramatic, don't you think?" she said, not bothering to look up from the butter she was churning.

"We don't even have food for this next week. At this rate, it's looking like that's what our fate will be."

Eliza's heart dropped.

No. Surely he was wrong. Surely this would all blow over soon, and she'd at least have the back half of her getaway to herself.

She'd go insane before she starved to death.

Granted, they did have milk, eggs, bread, and an endless stock of baking supplies. They wouldn't actually starve, but even Eliza needed something other than pastries and breakfast food to survive on.

"Maybe try the back door," Eliza suggested, eager to send him away. He'd been able to open it yesterday, moments before Puffcake flew inside.

"Good idea." He crossed the room to the back door, moving slowly to avoid any knee injuries from the kitchen this time. Just as he was about to pull on the peppermint handle, the deadbolt magically clicked into place.

Locked.

The house seemed to shudder a laugh.

Lachlan even tried unlatching a window. The latches snapped shut no sooner than after he unlocked them.

"Maybe there's a killer on the loose," Eliza suggested. "It's trying to keep us safe from them."

She dared not say that just yesterday, she even questioned if Lachlan was one himself. She really needed to stop watching so much true crime.

A knock came at the front door.

They just stared at each other from across the room. Even Puffcake lifted his head from where he lay on the mantle.

Eliza didn't want to answer, and if it had been any other week, she would've let whoever was at the door just stand there waiting in the cold. But she wanted to see if the door would open. Plus, it might've been the rental company coming to sort out the misunderstanding.

The thought made her quickly drop what she was doing and make a break for the door.

Eliza gently twisted the handle for fear that the magic might recognize her touch and recoil. Astonished, the door unlatched and slid open without a problem, like it wasn't possible for anything to cause it to be malfunctioning in the first place.

A woman about Eliza's age stood there, mid-length lavender hair tumbling around her face in ribbons. The lime-green snowsuit she wore made her eyes pop all the brighter. They were an unnatural-looking yellow-green, and she wore earmuffs that perfectly matched her suit, like she color-coordinated down to the last eccentric detail.

"Hi there! I'm Gretel. My brother, Hansel, and I live

in the cabin just down the road." She smiled widely, extending her hand in a formal greeting.

"Pleasure to meet you," Eliza said, shaking Gretel's hand back.

"Was offered free residence for life after an incident that happened in one of the cottages as kids," Gretel explained. "Anyways, I came by to invite you to the Reindeer Games in a couple of days, and figured, since you were renting this place during the week of Christmas, that you might like to know about them."

Before Eliza could kindly reject the offer, Lachlan came by her side. He lounged in the doorway, like the frame was made for him to wade in.

"Hi, Gretel," he greeted her with a smile. "We'd love to go."

"Except we can't," Eliza added on, looking at Lachlan in silent warning. "The snow is too high. We might get lost in all this."

Blaming it on the weather seemed better than flat out saying, *I don't want to go,* or, *our door magically locks on us and we don't want to be on the outside of it when it does.*

She'd be fine if the door magically jammed again, only this time with Lachlan on the *outside*. Puffcake could stay.

Gretel frowned. "Hansel and I would be happy to help shovel your driveway. All of the main roads are already clear. There's a shorter way to the village, too, in case you didn't pack proper winter gear."

The oven dinged, and Lachlan was already moving to pull the desserts out of the oven before Eliza could.

"It's also a great place to buy your husband a Christmas present," Gretel leaned in.

Behind her, Lachlan snorted.

"Oh," Eliza blushed. "He's not my husband. I'd really love to attend but … I don't want to get lost."

"Nonsense. Hansel lays out breadcrumbs all along the route for the visitors. So you really don't have an excuse," she winked, recognizing Eliza's reasoning for what they were: avoidance.

Lachlan approached again with a steaming pan of Eggnog Pudding. "Would you like to come inside and have a slice? We've been bored out of our minds with this weather and all. And Eliza's been baking quicker than we can eat it."

Puffcake glanced from his spot on the mantle with an expression that said, "*Speak for yourself.*"

Once again, Eliza failed to speak her objection before Gretel piped up: "I'd love to!" She smiled brightly, her teeth glistening like the snow behind her.

Great, Eliza thought. *Now we'll have even more people locked inside this Airbnb with us.*

Eliza turned, leading the way inside and shooting Lachlan a deadly glare. He smiled mischievously, knowing exactly what he did.

"Never been in here before, but have always wanted to," Gretel said, stealing a look about the place. "It's the perfect getaway, isn't it?"

Was, Eliza thought, but nodded instead.

"Sort of. You see ..." Eliza leaned over the island. "We've kind of been locked inside."

Gretel smiled. "You won't have to worry about that. I've already texted Hansel. He's on his way over now with a couple of shovels."

Eliza's mouth gaped open. She didn't know whether she should feel grateful or irritated. "Th-thank you," she croaked. "But I don't just mean because of the snow. This house ... it's ..."

"Haunted?" Gretel attempted to finish Eliza's sentence, her brow raised.

Eliza flinched at Gretel's word, knowing that the cottage was capable of listening, in its own way. "Well, the word I was going to say was enchanted, but—"

"It's a matter of perspective," Lachlan called, the sarcasm practically dripping off his tone.

Eliza ground her teeth. Was Lachlan suggesting the cottage was haunted because *she* was there? She made great company. If anyone was going to be trapped in a cottage mid-snowstorm, Eliza made the perfect candidate.

One: She was an excellent baker. Two: she didn't wish to converse, and three: she kept her quarter-life existential dread to herself, thank you very much.

Eliza opened the cabinet drawer with more force than necessary. The silverware, which was a set of peppermint sticks, rattled around.

Hearing the jingle, Puffcake woke from his stupor

and flapped his sugary wings over to the island to join the rest of them. Gretel greeted him with a squeal, interrupting the conversation to fawn over how cute he was. She reached out a hand—

"Don't boop him on the nose!" Eliza warned her.

Puffcake seemed pleased that Eliza remembered. Gretel stroked his spine instead, and he softly began to purr, settling into her lap as she continued petting him.

"Careful. We don't know if he melts." Lachlan said.

"Too late," Eliza snorted with amusement. Puffcake was now fully splayed across Gretel's lap, belly up, cinnamon-tongue hanging out and all.

Eliza scooped up a serving of the pudding, giving Puffcake half the amount she did the humans. He took one look at the bowl and then to Eliza, letting her know that he noticed and he was not pleased.

She gave him a pointed look. "You're about five inches tall and almost entirely made of sugar."

Puffcake just flicked his tail, blowing smoke through his nostrils.

Each of them dug in.

"Santa's beard!" Gretel let out. "This is *amazing*. It's like Christmas in a bowl."

"She's pretty incredible, isn't she?" Lachlan agreed. Eliza blushed at his comment, even though she knew he was speaking on behalf of her baking skills. "By the end of the week, I'm going to be rolling out of this gingerbread house."

Finishing off the pudding, Lachlan stretched out his

arms. "I'm going to head upstairs and do some reading until Hansel gets here, if the house will let me." Then his chocolate eyes landed on Eliza. She suddenly didn't know what to do with her hands. "Try not to burn down the kitchen while I'm away."

"I won't," Eliza rolled her eyes. "I bake things other than frozen pizzas, remember?"

Lachlan laughed, already halfway up the stairs. "Yeah, yeah."

Eliza caught herself smiling. Gretel just stared at Eliza suspiciously. Gretel lifted a perfectly arched lavender brow. "Not your boyfriend, huh?"

Eliza shook her head, her cheeks growing in warmth.

"Hmm," was all Gretel said, before scooting closer in her chair, her unnaturally green eyes wide with enthusiasm. "You should enter the baking contest at the Reindeer Games festival! I'd bet my bottom you'd win first place."

"There's a baking contest there?" Eliza asked.

Gretel, whose mouth was now full of the pudding, only nodded vigorously. She politely put her hand to her lips as she explained, "Every year. Same day, same sort of chaos, but in a different font. Usually, the prize comes down to either Frank or Mrs. Elle Toe."

"Mrs. Elle Toe?" Eliza raised an eyebrow.

"She's a retired librarian. Bakes for fun, lives to read and gossip. Absolutely ruthless with a piping bag. Frank's family has been running Mendel's Confections since this village was built. Like, literally. He might be a thousand, but everyone's too afraid to ask. Mrs. Elle Toe would be thrilled to add some fresh blood to the competition. Frank, on the other hand, I can't say the same."

Eliza smiled. "In that case, I think I might actually be up for going."

"Good," Gretel beamed and brushed her lavender hair away from her heart-shaped face. Then, she paused, tilting her head thoughtfully. "What were we saying before, about the house? Oh, right. Haunted." She didn't whisper the word.

Eliza stiffened. She noted how the fire in the hearth paused mid-crackle, as if it was listening in.

"You're not the first couple to mention that this place does some pretty weird stuff," she took another bite as if she hadn't just dropped the biggest truth bomb there was. "Some things can be chalked up to coincidence. Other things ... not so much."

Eliza set down her fork, suddenly not craving any more pudding. "What have you heard?"

"Just little stuff, mostly. The cupboard doors wouldn't open, the recipe books would vanish, or the words would disappear right off the page. One couple claimed that the sugar kept spilling onto the floor and wrote different words in it when they weren't looking. Others say the oven burns things, refusing to bake."

Eliza's thoughts hinged on the part where Gretel mentioned the recipe books, though none of the words ever vanished for her. The recipes glowed every time she looked through them, and the enchanted cookbook practically opened itself for Eliza. It even fell off the shelf to get her attention.

But with the oven refusing to bake, the doors locking on their own, and not allowing Lachlan out of her sight, it all tracked perfectly.

"Odd," was all Eliza said.

"It is." Gretel nodded in agreement. "And the weirdest part? The house doesn't do it to everyone. Only the couples staying here."

"But we're not a couple," Eliza reiterated.

"Like … at all?" Gretel asked, incredulous.

Eliza shook her head.

Gretel gave it some thought, scraping the last of the pudding off her plate. Puffcake nudged her hand with his frosted nose, clearly annoyed that she had stopped rubbing him. She scratched behind his ear absent-mindedly.

"I'm not really an expert on how the house oper-ates, but from what I've gathered, it seems like it usually happens to those with unresolved tension. Or, at the very least, attraction."

Eliza's stomach felt heavy, and she immediately blamed the pudding.

"I mean," Gretel went on, "maybe the house can sense when some things are being avoided. The magic's not exactly subtle."

Eliza blew out a breath. "You can say that again. All I wanted this Christmas holiday was to come here, bake, and spend all week avoiding my responsibilities. Then, I showed up to find that this place had been double-booked. The house even forces us together, so we have to be around each other."

Gretel flicked a dollop of pudding off her snowsuit, not seeming surprised in the slightest. "That's the frustrating thing about magic. It doesn't always make sense, but it makes you squirm like crazy until you find out the hard way."

"I'll agree to that, but I'm not …" Eliza lowered her voice. "I'm not … *attracted* to him." Even to Eliza, her voice didn't sound convincing.

Gretel, seeming unconvinced as well, simply crossed her arms. "Remember to tell that to the mistletoe when it hangs over your head."

"Mistletoe?" Eliza blinked, searching the rafters. "What mistletoe?"

Gretel just smiled. "You'll see." Without explanation, she checked her mobile. "Oh, jolly! Hansel's almost here. You got any proper winter boots?"

Eliza nodded. "In my car with the rest of my bags. I'll need help shoveling the snow off my car to get them out."

"No worries. I'll text Hansel to tell him to get them out now for you, along with your luggage."

"T-thank you," Eliza stuttered out. Why was Gretel being so nice to her? She wasn't used to this kind of treatment.

Gretel waved her off, saying, "Don't worry about it," but Eliza couldn't help but still feel like a burden.

"Um. Gretel?" Eliza called after her. "Do you happen to know the cottage's Wi-Fi code? My phone signal here is rubbish."

A knock came at the door. Only a head of navy hair was visible from where Eliza sat at the island. Gretel rose from her seat in a peppermint-scented wind and headed for the door.

"WirelessWonderland225," she said before turning the doorknob to let her brother inside.

Chapter Six

Christmas Spirit

Eliza really wasn't sure if she was okay with this many people in her cottage. And yes, technically, it wasn't just *hers*, but after baking two batches of puff-cakes, midnight merengues, red velvet biscuits, Eggnog pudding, and emotionally unpacking in every room, she felt entitled to being territorial.

She supposed she didn't have much of a choice. Hansel and Gretel were going to help shovel the snow from the driveway, which meant she *had* to allow them inside to do some awkward small talk, or at the very least, allow them to linger on the front porch and offer them a cup of hot chocolate.

She trudged up the stairs, along with her bags, which Hansel pulled from her car, to get Lachlan. She felt a tinge of satisfaction knowing that she was disturbing him. She didn't wait for a "come in" after she knocked.

But the joke was on her, because Lachlan was sitting there shirtless.

"Oop—" she chirped, yanking on the door to shut it. But the door wouldn't budge. Suddenly, it felt like it weighed two tons. She put all her might into it, but … nothing. Clearly, the house was scheming.

She gave up, refusing to look anywhere but the bed. She focused her attention on the white chocolate trim, intensely intrigued by its design. "Hansel's here. They're going to start shoveling outside. Thought you might want to help."

Lachlan shut his laptop and stretched, his muscles flexing. "Nah. I'd rather make the two siblings do all the dirty work. What are their names again? Pancake and Kettle?"

"Hansel and Gretel." Eliza reiterated, crossing her arms. "Be nice. They can't help their names. Besides, you're one to talk. What's Lachlan mean, anyways?"

She left out the part that she was genuinely curious, not just wanting to reprimand him for making fun of the siblings' names.

"It's Irish for the Land of the Lakes. It's a family name, even though none of us are Irish."

"Is that so?"

He nodded. "British as they come. What about you?"

Eliza shrugged. "I've never really asked. My mum's from London and my dad is from Oxford. They met at university. Have been inseparable ever since."

Lachlan seemed to consider this for a moment, lip twitching upwards slightly. "Figured you'd be from the North Pole yourself, with your baking skills and all."

She laughed. A real, unexpected one.

Magical gingerbread house, indeed.

"I have my nan to thank for that. My family would come here every Christmas for as long as I can remember. She was the one who taught me how to bake."

"All hail Nan Snow." Lachlan playfully raised and lowered his hands in a gesture of praise. "Why didn't they book it this year?" he asked.

"We stopped coming since she died," she swallowed, her throat seizing up all of a sudden. The tears always felt just behind her eyes and ready to spill anytime she had to vocalize the truth—the reality of what had happened this past spring that she was too afraid to think about.

"I'm terribly sorry to hear that." Then, he quirked a brow, a silent question. "But you're still here."

She exhaled sharply, still not willing to meet his eyes. "Needed some space to clear my head. Not just because of her death." She diverted the conversation away from her nan, being more willing to discuss her recent heartbreak than her. Even though she was torn over the loss of the bakery and breakup, she knew she'd eventually recover. The loss of Nan, however, she was certain she'd never fully recover.

"It was because of a breakup," she continued, saving herself the humiliation of his asking.

But it was much more than that. It was a broken-off engagement. A lost business. Six years down the drain because of a reconnection with an old "mate."

Silence stretched between them, like he was waiting for her to explain more, but that was all she was willing to give. And she certainly wasn't going to ask why *he* was here. She was just eager to shovel this snow, get him settled in another place, and drown herself in biscuits and tears. Alone.

"My sister said I work too much this time of year," he said finally. "So she booked me a getaway to spend through the week to hopefully find some Christmas spirit." He forced out an exaggerated breath. "Whatever that means."

"It means you're a Scrooge," she blurted.

Lachlan looked offended. "Would a Scrooge wear Christmas socks?"

"If he was trying to fool others," she shot back.

"Oh, so what, I'm a phony Christmas boy who wears cheesy socks for no reason?"

"Yes," she said. "Yes, that's exactly it. You're a wolf in sheep's clothing."

They stared down at each other, eyes playful, and both nearly breaking into a smile. And the tension between them thawed just a little. He swung his feet over the edge of the bed and stood, flexing his bare chest. Eliza made herself busy by inspecting the Advent calendar on the wall.

Would you look at that? Five more days until Christmas.

It'd be her first one spent without her nan. Without any family, including Davis and his less-than-charming mother. She couldn't say she was upset with missing the Hall family Christmas dinner, but she was struck with a small pinch of guilt when she thought about how she wouldn't be at her own family gathering this year either.

The pain was too much. She didn't feel like spending it anywhere else than where it was supposed to be: here, in this very cottage.

On his way out the door, flannel in hand, Lachlan stopped beside her. He stooped down to meet her eyes and ever-so-gently lifted her chin with his thumb. "You okay, Snow?"

His brown eyes were downturned, his eyebrows furrowed slightly. There was an expression that Eliza knew to be sincere. He actually seemed to care.

She only nodded, plastering on a smile.

Though he seemed unconvinced, Lachlan didn't push. He only traveled down the stairs and out the back door to help the siblings. When she heard the door shut behind him, she took a moment, blinking back tears as she sat on the bed. Just a moment. She closed her eyes.

The house was quiet. Only the faint hum of the

hearth. The groans of the gingerbread beams as they settled, the drip-drip-drip of the ice melting from the rooftop.

Solitude at last.

She was thankful to the magical Airbnb that it allowed her this time, if only just this once. It was like it knew she needed it, and put its antics on the back burner for the time being so she could finally sit with her thoughts.

She lay back and pulled the patchwork quilt over her head, cocooning herself in the warm scent of gingerbread mixed with the sharpness of evergreen. Eliza grumbled. Could she not even have this moment not to be reminded of Lachlan's presence?

Reaching for her mobile, she typed in the Wi-Fi code Gretel had given her earlier and waited for the signal to kick in. Her phone lit up like Piccadilly Circus.

Ding. Ding. Ding, ding, ding, ding, ding.

Fifteen missed calls. Twelve unread texts. Most from her best friend, Piper, but a few from her mum.

She clicked on her mum's name first.

> Did you make it there, sweetheart?

> *a picture of a pair of hideous leather boots*

> Do you like these, darling? Thinking of ideas to get you for Christmas.

> Piper texted me to ask if I'd heard from you. Are you okay?

And just now.

Call me!!!

Before she could hit the call button, the phone started ringing. She answered, and the sound of her mum's voice came through the other end, half-relieved and half-panicked.

"Eliza? Oh, Thank God! I was two seconds away from calling the police to file a report. Did you make it there okay?"

Eliza smiled despite herself. "Yes, mum. I made it. There's no service here and I got snowed in. But I'm fine."

Long story short.

Her mum inhaled a soft, motherly breath. "Are you enjoying your time so far?"

She swallowed. She thought of Puffcake. Lachlan. Hansel. Gretel. The magical cookbook and nostalgic moments in the kitchen. It wasn't all bad, per se. Just not what she initially expected.

"It's complicated." She tried to make it sound humorous, but it just came out pathetic and sad.

"Oh, sweetheart. I miss you so much. I just wish you had stayed home with us."

Eliza gritted her teeth. No. If it had all gone according to plan, she would've had a fine week here. She wouldn't have to share a house with sheets that smelled like him. The house wouldn't literally be trying to matchmake the two of them. She'd be one of the blissful singles who stayed here, problem-free.

Just the magical kitchen and herself.

"It's okay. I'm getting a lot of baking done. In fact, I have a batch of biscuits in the oven," she fibbed. "Can I call you later?"

"Sure. Just glad you're there, safe. I love you," she said.

"I love you, too. Bye-bye."

Eliza moved on to the next contact: Piper.

So many white bubbles. She scrolled to the top, reading each short message:

is your murderer fit, at least?

???

oh God Eliza please tell me this is a joke

ELIZA

if you don't answer me back in 5 seconds I'm going to call your mum

called your mum. she said signal there's rubbish. we're trying not to panic but

honestly, if someone was going to kill you, it would be a place without signal

PICK UP YOUR PHONE ASAP

The mobile barely rang before Piper answered, her

high soprano voice breaking through. "Elizabeth Jane Snow!" she exploded. "You're *alive*? I was two seconds away from making a missing person's TikTok account!"

"I'm fine," Eliza laughed. "I didn't mean to ghost you, my phone's had no signal. I got snowed in, and— " she tried to explain.

"You didn't *just* ghost me. You left me on read, and then haunted my ever-waking thoughts until you answered. I was just starting to plan your funeral playlist!"

Eliza snorted, seeming genuinely cheered up. Leave it to Piper for that. "Let me guess. Lots of Taylor Swift and Adele on loop?"

"Of course. Festive, but also respectfully tasteful." Piper paused. "But enough about your funeral—we won't need the playlist for a few more years, hopefully. Since you never answered earlier ... *is* he fit?"

Eliza rolled her eyes. Her friend sounded like one of those girls in the movies who curled the cord in their finger as they gossiped on an old landline. "He's not hard on the eyes, and I think he knows it."

"Tell me everything right now! Who is he? Is he single? Is he the Airbnb host? A lost hiker? A Hallmark lumberjack?"

"He's none of those, unfortunately." Eliza blew out a breath. "Except for the single part, I'm not sure about that." She thought for a moment. Surely no one in a serious relationship with someone would take a week-long trip by themselves, especially during Christmas.

"He's staying here with me. The Airbnb was double-booked."

Piper squealed so loud that Eliza had to remove her ear from the phone. "This is a Hallmark knockoff at the minimum! This gives a "hard launch winter romance" vibe all the way. Imagine how many likes you'd get from TikTok on a story like this!"

She groaned. "It's nothing but a hard launch migraine, trust me."

Piper ignored her. "Does he chop wood? He totally chops wood, doesn't he?"

Eliza glanced out the window, seeing him shoveling in the distance, flannel underneath his coat and all. "He burned a frozen pizza. Does that count?"

She was *not* about to tell her that the house was magical and tried forcing the two of them together whenever it got the chance.

"Oh no," Piper gasped. "He's *damaged*. You can fix him. No, really, you can."

"I'm not fixing *anyone*, Piper. I just want to be alone." She rolled onto her side, letting her voice drop. "He's not terrible. We're just mostly annoyed with each other by the circumstances."

"That's absolutely what someone in love would say," Piper said.

Eliza didn't respond.

Piper let out a sigh. "Well, sometimes good things can come from the unexpected. You deserve good."

Eliza's throat tightened, and she sat up. That was her

cue to hang up. "Hey, I gotta go. The oven just went off. Burning some biscuits as we speak!"

"Love you! Send me hourly updates. I want all the deets. The longing stares, the mistletoe kisses, the snow-ball fights. Now that I'm fairly positive you're not going to get murdered, I'm living vicariously through you."

"Love you too," Eliza giggled. "Bye." She shook her head, clicking the red "end" button.

Eliza still had one more unread message. From Davis.

> I'm sorry you felt hurt last week, but I think my motives were misinterpreted. You know the business was always safest in my hands. I was the one with all the ideas, anyway. I put in so much time and effort for you, more than anyone else would've, and it still didn't seem like enough. It was just so exhausting trying to prove myself to someone who doesn't appreciate everything I've done. Enjoy your getaway. Hopefully, you'll get some closure. It's for the best this way.

Eliza's hands shook as she read the text, a pit forming at the base of her stomach.

One day, she'd know how much she dodged a bullet. But right now, it was hard not to wonder if he was right. If she truly was the problem. If the business truly was better left to Davis.

Honeycomb. That had been the name of the bakery

she started. The nickname her nan gave her one tiring, sugar-filled day when Eliza was too short to see over the kitchen counter.

It hadn't just been a name. It'd been hers. *Theirs*, hers, and Nan's.

Not his.

She hadn't asked to keep it; she only asked for him *not* to keep it. But she didn't have the money to fight him, and Davis knew that. He would've dragged out the legal battle long enough to let her desperation show, until her resolve thinned out.

The victory for him wasn't about taking the name— it was about knowing he took it because he *could*. The power. It was just another thing he'd taken from her.

Eliza blinked hard and deleted the message. She wouldn't cry about this again. It would've been the thousandth time, and this trip was to get away. While she was thinking about it, she blocked his number.

Good flipping riddance.

Eliza changed her clothes, stepping out of Lachlan's joggers and into jeans and a butter yellow sweater. She pulled on her thick wool socks and Uggs and headed downstairs.

At the foot of the staircase, Puffcake looked like a frosted gargoyle as he sat next to the mantle. Her heart twitched just a little. Had he waited for her?

He looked up at her, letting out tiny puffs of smoke as he danced in a circle.

"Yeah, I'm ready too. Let's go."

Eliza opened the back door, and Puffcake sprang like a shotgun out of its barrel and into the cold.

Chapter Seven

The Snowball Fight

Unsurprisingly, the door didn't even groan in protest as Eliza walked through the threshold. She felt like she was a spy in some movie, sneaking past all the loaded tripwires.

The bright light reflecting off the snow caused her to squint.

In the raised garden beds were swirling peppermints and brightly colored candy that resembled flowers blanketed in snow.

She noticed how untouched this section of the cottage was, and for a moment she paused. It was quiet, too quiet.

She didn't even hear the grating of the shovels against pavement as the siblings and Lachlan worked.

Behind her, Puffcake let out a loud bark, startling her. She turned to see what the matter was before—

Splat.

A perfectly round, perfectly cold snowball hit her cheek, bursting into tiny flakes. She looked down at her clothes, stunned, seeing that they were completely soaked.

Gretel's laugh flitted through the air. Eliza decided she couldn't be mad. If it were Lachlan, it would've been a completely different story.

"I told her not to do it," said a man standing next to her. Hansel casually propped a hand against his shovel, an apologetic smile on his face.

He wore a black and white checkered sweater and a red vest, seeming unbothered by the freezing temperature. Navy blue hair peeked out from his beanie, his features a faint echo of Gretel's, only sharper and more pronounced. But their eyes were the same shade of deep purple.

Beside him, Gretel didn't look the least bit sorry. She laughed as she packed another bundle of snow, and this time, Eliza ducked. But it wasn't aimed at her.

Puffcake let out a yelp. A mound of snow lay on the ground, smoke sizzling from within. He burst out of it and came up swinging and hissing.

He flew over to hide behind Eliza's shoulder, looking wounded.

"Don't do that," Lachlan warned Gretel. "He might get all soggy."

Puffcake let out a huff like he agreed.

Lachlan came over to dust a speck of snow off of Puffcake's snout. Eliza's eyes caught his, and she was reminded of the way he stood in front of her, pulling her chin upwards to meet his gaze.

Eliza turned to the cinnamon flamethrower and faked another smile. At this point, it felt effortless. "Puffcake, are you thinking what I'm thinking?"

Puffcake didn't have eyebrows, but if he had, Eliza knew he'd have them raised, egging her on to avenge their attacks.

Gretel ducked behind the garden bed for cover. She lifted her head, a lavender bun poking up from the top, and Eliza threw with all the force she could muster.

Snow pelted Gretel's ivory skin. She wiped her face clean, cheeks rosy, and whooped a laugh.

"We really should get back to work," Eliza said, breathlessly. Though she couldn't deny that her time had been fun, she was eager to get back to baking. In solitude, hopefully sometime soon, after she helped shovel the rest of the snow.

Then she looked to the front of the house to find a heap of snow piled high on either side of the driveway. Even their cars had been defrosted. Done already? How long had she been inside?

"You know what these piles would be good for?" Gretel's smile grew slowly across her face. "Snowball fight forts! C'mon, boys against girls. Puffcake can be the referee."

Eliza bit her lip. How could she break the news kindly to her? "Thanks, but I—"

"We need to get going," Lachlan interrupted. He briefly looked at Eliza before adjusting his hat and starting off through the snow to his Land Rover. "We need to get in touch with the rental company. See what's the matter."

Eliza followed, half-heartedly bracing herself to say her goodbyes. But the moment Lachlan unlocked his car, the wind picked up.

At first, it was just a little breeze. Then it grew into a loud, howling scream. The wind spun harder and harder. Hansel lost his beanie, and Puffcake flapped his wings vigorously against the wind, trying not to get sucked up into it.

Sugar-dusted wind whipped past their faces, and Eliza's hair stuck to her lap balm. The heaps of snow piled high on the driveway were caught up in the tornado of snow and wind. Then—

Whomp!

The wind ceased. The snow piles collapsed just at the end of the driveway, sparkling like a solid wall of ice.

A second later, the candy cane street lamp flickered like it'd been possessed.

Once, twice. A third time.

Lachlan and Eliza stared. He seemed to be at a loss for words. "Um. Was that—"

"Normal?" Gretel smiled, looking thrilled. "Oh, the house likes you two."

"What do you mean by 'like'?" Eliza asked.

"Like—*like, like*," Gretel's eyes sparkled with mischief. "Means it's not going to let either of you leave until it's ready."

"Happens sometimes," Hansel added. "Usually, when two people are being stubborn."

Puffcake fluttered up to the sheet of ice and barked at it like a guard dog.

Lachlan let out a frustrated sigh, the vapors visible in the chilly winter air. "Did you ever hear back from the host, Eliza?"

Her face fell. She'd honestly forgotten to check. Between enchanted ovens and limitless pantries, a house not-so-subtly match-making the two of them, and phone calls from home, it'd slipped her mind entirely.

Picking up her phone, she opened the booking app. The real one—not MagicalStays, the app she'd initially used to reserve the booking. She typed up a quick message, like a signal flare for help.

Good afternoon! I booked the cottage 2424 Drury Lane through MagicalStays, and it looks like the property has been double-booked. I want to check in to see if there's any way one of us could be relocated, especially with the holiday coming up. Thanks so much! -Eliza

"Well, in the meantime, we might as well have some fun," Gretel said, packing a snowball with the practice of an expert.

"Can we shoot at the referee?" Lachlan asked, eyeballing Puffcake.

Puffcake blew a warning cloud of smoke, taking a seat on top of a rock shaped like a marshmallow. The message was clear: referee immunity.

Without warning, Hansel yelled, "One, two, three, *go*!" He rained down snowballs on Eliza and Gretel. The girls yelped before sprinting around the side of the house as the powdery explosions showered down on them.

They skidded around the corner and hit the snow on their knees. Gretel moved at lightning speed, already creating more ammunition.

Eliza peeked around the corner. "They're gaining on us!"

When she turned back around, she blinked. A mound of perfectly round snowballs now sat a few paces beside them. Gretel followed her gaze and laughed.

"Did the house just *arm us*?" Eliza asked.

"Guess it did."

They both pounced around the house, rapid-firing them off like Buddy the Elf in Central Park. Lachlan ducked for cover, clearly outmatched. The house's gutter tilted, dumping an entire stash on his head. The girls laughed, high-fiving each other in triumph.

The house creaked its laughter, too, and the gutter righted itself.

Puffcake raised a candy cane, waving it in the air like a flag. "*Round two*."

A notification from SugarPlum Suites popped up, and Eliza immediately slid her phone unlocked to read the message.

> Hi there! Unfortunately, since you both booked through third-party sites it seems we accidentally booked you for the same stay. We're terribly sorry for the inconvenience. Due to the holiday week, there is no additional housing at this time. However, we can offer both of you complimentary stays for your next visit to SugarPlum Suites. Happy Holidays!

"So, I guess that means we're stuck here for Christmas." Eliza let out a puff of air, her shoulders sagging. She passed her phone around for the others to read.

Eliza crossed her arms, her throat tightening. She didn't want a complimentary stay for next year—she wanted the stay she paid for *this* year. Now that her entire stay had been ruined, she didn't feel like doing anything other than trudging back into the kitchen and getting back to work.

Gretel's eyes skimmed over the words, but she didn't seem too surprised by the response. "Guess so. But Hansel and I could've told you that."

"Totally normal Airbnb behavior," Eliza groaned, dropping her hands to her sides.

Gretel laughed. "You both are, like, honorary locals now. Which means you'll *have* to attend the Reindeer Games. On Christmas Eve Eve."

Eliza surveyed Gretel. "Even if I wanted to go, *how* would I?" Wasn't the house trapping her inside at all costs? She didn't feel like getting excited about anything for fear that someone might pull the rug out from underneath her feet once again.

The siblings exchanged looks as Gretel beamed. "Because I already entered you into the baking contest."

"*What*?" Eliza gaped. "Why would you do that?"

"Because you're the best baker the town's never heard of," Gretel said, pointing a finger at her chest. "And we're gonna get you that first-place prize."

"Which is?"

"Five thousand quid."

Eliza's heart nearly stopped. Puffcake accidentally coughed fire out of his mouth.

For a friendly neighborhood competition?

That wouldn't be enough to start her own business, but it'd certainly give her a head start.

She was breathless. "Then I ... I need to practice!"

"So that means you'll do it?" Gretel asked enthusiastically.

"Of course!" Eliza said, already dusting off the snow from her coat as she headed inside. "Thank you both for helping us clear the driveway. Even if it was for nothing."

"It wasn't for nothing," Hansel shook his head. "We were happy to help."

Gretel smiled and gave a small shrug. "And anyway, everything happens for a reason."

Chapter Eight

Baking Ad-Lib

I'll be Home for Christmas Clementine and Cointreau Mince Pies

Ingredients:

- *8oz Plain Flour*
- *Pinch Of Salt*
- *6oz Butter (if butter is scarce, good baking margarine will do nicely)*
- *3oz Caster Sugar*
- *1 Egg Yolk (Save the egg white for glazing or tomorrow's breakfast)*

• Mum's Mincemeat (which is top secret, but you can find it in the cupboard)
• Zest of Clementines
• 2 tbsp Cointreau

1. Preheat the oven to 190°C. Grease mince pie tin.
2. Combine ingredients except the zest, Cointreau, and mince meat until it resembles breadcrumbs. No machinery required! Just sing to the tune of "I'll be Home for Christmas" to mix.
3. Chill the pastry for 10 minutes.
4. Tip mincmeat into a bowl. Stir in zest of clementine and Cointreau.
5. Roll out the dough, cut, and line the tins.
6. Fill with mincemeat. Cut star shapes from the remaining pastry and place on top of each pie.
7. Bake for around 20 minutes until golden and bubbling.

She swallowed, eyes catching on step number two. She was unsure if she should risk singing at this hour. What if she woke Lachlan? More importantly, what if he woke up to find her *singing* to the batter?

Then he'd really think she'd lost her marbles.

Whatever. She would pretend she was alone, put the consequences in a stocking, and shove it up the chimney.

She murmured the song, her eyes on the grandfather clock. Lachlan shifted, and Puffcake lifted his head, unamused. He huffed powdered sugar, stretched, and curled up again.

It was the longest minute of her life, but she finished the notes, the batter shifting from a pale yellow to a spectacular shade of cream. It seemed to sparkle with enthusiasm.

As it baked, her stomach growled. Smelling the crisp scent of the fruit mixed with the sweetness of the batter, she grew impatient to try it.

In the meantime, she decided to check her mobile to see if she could find any information online about the baking competition. Clicking onto the SugarPlum Suites app and tapping on the "events" tab, a bright pink flyer popped across her screen.

She saw the Reindeer Game's information with fun add-ons like a biscuit swap table, caroling, DIY snow globes, ice carving exhibits, and more. A little lower, she scrolled to see it.

Baking Spirits Bright Guidelines:
•All entries must be homemade and prepped from scratch.
•Entries should be dropped off no later than 5:00 pm on December 23rd. The tasting festivities will begin at 5:30 pm sharp, and the winner will be announced shortly after.
•Recipes will be requested for transparency and for sharing in the local newspaper.

The guidelines didn't say anything about magically inspired recipes, but she wasn't sure if this was something she'd like to share with the world. Using Isadora's recipes felt deeply personal. If this cottage had wanted to share them with just anyone, it would've by now.

Deciding against using one of Isadora's, Eliza scrolled through Pinterest instead. She looked for Christmas dishes that seemed equally as appealing as the ones inside the cookbook, but there wasn't anything that stood out to her. After several minutes, she locked her phone, tightened her apron, and brainstormed the old-fashioned way.

She liked to call it her Baking Ad-Lib:

Two ingredients for flavor. One ingredient for texture and one for visual appeal.

The timer on her mobile rang out, and she took out the pie from the oven. Now she just needed to wait for it to cool. She thought to make herself busy as she strode around the kitchen, blindly choosing the ingredients she could use for the contest.

Eliza couldn't explain it, she just followed her baking intuition. She'd inherited this trait from her nan, who always said intuition was half of what made an excellent baker. When all other wells of inspiration ran dry, she always knew when to trust her gut. And her taste buds.

From the top shelf, she pulled down cranberries. Good, that would be one of her flavors. Bonus points for its visual appeal and texture. For her other flavor, she chose orange slices, for the way it complemented the cranberries.

Scones, she thought. *Perfect*.

She plucked a pie off the rack for herself, the steam rising into the air. Her mouth watered, eager to taste, but also to test if she would have another memory.

In the first bite, she tasted the sweetness of the sugar mixed with the bite of bitterness, brief but still present. She blinked, and in an instant, she was taken back. Another time, but the same place.

A Christmas tree sat in the corner, the smell of fresh evergreen and sap filling the cottage. Balancing on a stool was the same girl with onyx hair. *Isadora*.

Today, she was dressed in a bright 1950s red gingham midi dress. She looked like a cottage princess with half of her hair pulled back in a matching bow.

Like last time, Ernest approached from behind. He lifted Isadora at her tiny waist and twirled her down to the ground. Somewhere in the background, a vintage-sounding "*I'll Be Home For Christmas*" played over the record player in a slow melody.

"Hey now," her husband said, giving her another playful spin. "Told you I would hang the star on the tree."

"I know," Isadora smiled. "But I was eager to see it all come together." They swayed together like this, looking into each other's eyes. They didn't speak much. They were together. They let their bodies do the communicating as they swayed around and around, the only light coming from the tree.

Isadora smiled up at Ernest, gazing at him like he'd hung the moon. "You came back from your walk at the perfect time. I have a surprise for you."

"Oh?" Ernest's eyebrows raised in anticipation, searching Isadora's tiny frame for any physical changes. "Any news yet?"

Her smile faltered for a fraction of a second:

The oven chimed a familiar ding, and Isadora's smile flashed bright again. She floated into the kitchen and pulled on a pair of oven mitts.

Instead of matching her excitement, Ernest rolled his eyes when Isadora wasn't looking. He reluctantly followed after her into the kitchen, leaning against the counter. "Another sweet? Really, honey?"

Isadora opened the oven and set the pie down on the island. It smelled of baked surprises and hopeful dreams.

"Mince Pie!" she chirped. "Your favorite."

She didn't seem to catch his hesitation to join her at the table. After cooling, she cut a slice and brought it over to the table. He just stood at the counter, nursing a cup of coffee. He'd picked up a stack of newspapers and began reading. Eliza caught the date: December 20th, 1945. Eighty years ago.

"Come sit with me, dear," Isadora pleaded, "all this dancing must've made you hungry, yeah?"

He lowered the newspaper just a touch to see over it.

He gave a distant smile. "Thank you, but I think I'll pass. I'm still full from your last baking escapade."

She blinked, her arms extended with his plate. "But you didn't have any of those, either."

"Sure, I did, honey. Just a few were plenty for me." He chuckled, but his tone was dismissive.

She withdrew, her thoughts turning pensive. "I'll just wrap it up for you, then … We can have it—"

"I said I didn't want any. What I want is a child!" Ernest's tone suddenly changed, and he slapped the paper down in his lap with a crunch. Isadora flinched back, covering her face. It was a subtle gesture, but both Eliza and Ernest caught it.

He didn't apologize for his outburst, only corrected it with a smile. Like that's all he would need to do to make everything else he did beforehand go away. "Let's not fight, honey. We came here to escape all of that, remember?"

Isadora's face fell for only a fraction of a second, but she caught it before Ernest could say anything. She sank on the sofa, looking at her hands with contempt.

On the record player, the lyrics began to slow as the memory lulled ...

"I'll be home for Christmas, if only in my dreams …"

A hollow silence hung between them, heavy and palpable. Then the song came to an abrupt end along with the memory. Eliza was back.

The memory clung to her like the steam of the pies

—fresh and warm yet laced with an undertone of bitterness.

Ernest had wanted a child. Was Isadora unwilling to give him one, or was she unable to? And if she'd wanted them, was it more complicated than that?

What if she were nervous about what kind of mother she'd be? Or was it that she was more nervous about what kind of father Ernest would be?

She couldn't help but feel sorry for Isadora, knowing that this was exactly how it started. The distance. The avoidance. The silent betrayals. The way someone you loved deeply seemed to slowly drift away while seated right beside you.

She knew it all, and watching it play out for someone else was like watching a sad film where you know one of the characters is betrayed at the end. You can't stop it from happening. You can only watch the tragedy unfold.

Eliza sighed; so many questions about this woman's life plagued her. She'd have to bake the rest of the memories to find out what happened in the end.

That's how, she guessed, it felt now, thinking back to her relationship with Davis. Everyone knew it was over before it even began unfurling. It was only a matter of time before he broke her heart and left her stranded trying to pick up the pieces. Piper had even tried to warn her, saying that he seemed too into himself, too absorbed with himself to truly care for anyone else.

Piper was right. She was always right.

Eliza drew in a breath, wiping a tear from her eye. She reached for her notepad, already tired of grieving over her own heartbreak. She didn't need the weight of someone else's too, even if it happened eighty years ago.

She rounded up each of her ingredients she'd chosen earlier: cranberries, orange zest, nutmeg, and a touch of cinnamon, and scribbled the title down onto the page. *Winter Hearth Scones*. It sounded comforting and bright, yet warm and, of course, delicious.

She hoped that if she could bake anything into this recipe, it would be hope. For herself. For Isadora. For Nan. For Honeycomb.

Lachlan snored softly on the couch, blissfully unaware of the spiritual breakthroughs happening in the kitchen right next to him. Even Puffcake stirred inside the bowl, letting out a tiny puff of powdered sugar.

Then, Eliza began baking, allowing the steady rhythm to calm her. She didn't know if she would win the contest, didn't know how things would end for Isadora. Didn't know if she was ready to love yet, or ever again. But she knew this: she believed in new beginnings.

Her scones would be proof of that.

Chapter Nine

Tree Therapy

Eliza could've baked all evening, but with the contest looming, she thought that getting a good night's rest was more prudent.

She woke to the rich smell of fresh coffee and bacon. Her stomach grumbled, and she allowed her hunger to carry her down the steps. Lachlan stood in the kitchen, his dark hair tousled from sleep, cooking with her mint green Christmas apron. He made it look like a festive hand towel wrapped around his tall, muscular frame.

At first, he didn't notice her, so she just stood

watching from behind as he flipped the bacon, the frying pan popping and sizzling under the heat.

Eliza quickly whipped out her phone to take a picture of him. The snap of her iPhone camera gave away her presence, and he turned, frowning at her. She grinned and snapped another, this time catching him full on and staring right into the camera, looking heavily amused.

"Like what you see?" he said with a smirk.

Eliza's cheeks reddened, not knowing how to answer. "Maybe. You do kinda look like someone from one of those sexy Christmas commercials. You know, like the ones where the male model is shirtless outside in the snow advertising for some restaurant?"

He raised a brow, leaning against the counter and mischievously popping out a hip. "So I'm a male model to you?"

Eliza realized her grave mistake a second too late but recovered it quickly, hiding the blush deepening on her cheeks by taking a sip of her coffee he had generously laid out on the table for her. "Don't let it get to your head. It's the apron doing all the heavy lifting."

He laughed, a warm melody that flooded her ears. It sounded like Christmas bells. He crossed his arms over his chest, biceps flexing. "Is that so? Maybe I'll lean into the whole culinary heartthrob angle. Pick myself up a hot model girlfriend along the way ..."

Her attention snagged on the *girlfriend* part. So he was single?

Not that Eliza was interested.

"Please," she snorted into her coffee. "I've seen better."

"Just admit it," his smile grew, teeth gleaming as white as marshmallows. He reached over her head to grab a plate. "You're going to be thinking about this long after Christmas." He gestured to the apron with his hands.

A dramatic retching sound came from the corner of the kitchen. Eliza jumped, sloshing her coffee. Puffcake peeked his icing-covered snout over the top of the mixing bowl, hanging out his tongue in disgust.

Lachlan chuckled, loading three plates of food. "The apron's a hard pass from Puffcake."

Puffcake breathed, and white powdery sugar sprang from his nostrils. He lowered his head back in the bowl.

"He's so judgmental in the mornings," Eliza said.

"Must get it from you," he said. He set their plates down on the round breakfast table, pulling out the seat for her. She also noted there was a tiny plate left on the windowsill for Puffcake, so he could eat his breakfast in luxury.

Eliza's heart wrenched, thinking of Isadora. Is this how it started for her, too? With sweet gestures and early morning breakfasts? With fresh coffee and easy flirting? Minus the sassy cinnamon-crusted dragon, of course.

She wrapped her hands around her coffee as she sat, enveloping herself in the warmth.

"Everything okay?" Lachlan's brows furrowed. Puffcake raised his head again from his current bed and slinked his way over, not skipping a beat as he gobbled up his food.

"Yeah," she sipped. "Just thinking."

Lachlan set the spatula down and splayed his hands out on either side of the table. "Funny you should mention it, because *I've* been thinking."

"Have you, now?" Eliza widened her eyes playfully. "Didn't know that was possible."

"Hilarious," he deadpanned. "I've been thinking we don't have a tree. And what's Christmas without a tree?"

Eliza had noticed it, too. The house certainly lacked a kind of charming glow without it. But she really didn't want to take away time from baking to go hunting for one, not when she was having these kinds of baking epiphanies. Already, she was eager to have Lachlan step aside so she could bake the three of them cinnamon rolls, American pancakes, *something* sweet to go alongside their meal.

She could do without a Christmas tree. Unless she wanted to pipe a few shortbread sugar biscuits shaped like Christmas trees and call it a day.

Eliza didn't respond. Sensing her apathy, Lachlan sighed. "Look, I'll be honest with you. This isn't the way I saw my Christmas being spent, either. If it were up to me, I wouldn't go get a tree at all, but … My sister says that I need to. That it would help …" he tried to find the right words, but couldn't seem to. "I don't know, I guess, cheer me up?"

What did he need so much cheering up about? If he were to ask her, she'd tell him that he cared too much about what his sister thought. If Lachlan's sister wanted him to do certain things, she should be here with him to do them.

Eliza arched a brow as Lachlan stumbled through his explanation. "So, what? Your sister thinks you need tree therapy, or something?"

"That's not a clinical term, but I believe so, yes."

"You could prove your Christmas spirit to your sister by telling her that you're stuck in an enchanted cottage with a gingerbread dragon and a girl who throws flour at you like a hand grenade."

"Yeah, I have a strong inclination that she wouldn't believe me. For good reason, too. But she *would* believe that I met someone, and we were going tree shopping together."

Eliza's heart took a leap. She wondered if he *would* tell his sister about her. The thought made her swell with pride a little.

Don't be silly, Eliza, it's just a joke.

"I don't know …" Eliza's voice trailed off, her enthusiasm—along with her confidence—waning.

"Puffcake can go too," he sing-songed.

Puffcake just huffed in response, and Lachlan looked hopeful.

"You really want to go get one, don't you?" Eliza asked, setting down her coffee.

"I could try to go alone, if the house would let me. Probably would just pick up a sad Charlie Brown tree. One with saggy limbs and wilting pine needles."

"Fine," she rolled her eyes. "I'll pick out the tree, but you're paying for it and carrying it back. I'm not about to be a part of the climate crisis."

"Deal. Like any of that was ever in question." He settled himself back in his chair, smiling brightly.

Her stomach flipped, but she blamed it on the caffeine.

Yesterday, Eliza had asked Gretel how they'd be able to find the road in the middle of this blizzard, and she'd simply responded with a smile. "Breadcrumbs," she'd said, but one thing Lachlan and Eliza didn't plan for was how the house might react to the two of them leaving, even if it was together.

She twisted the peppermint-striped knob, but like yesterday, the door didn't budge. "Darn, we'll just have to stay inside today …" Eliza said.

Lachlan shot her a look. "Maybe the house only lets us leave on its terms?" he jested.

She shrugged. "Your guess is as good as mine."

Puffcake's gumdrop eyes popped open, as if suddenly struck with an idea. He batted his little glittery wings over to them, using his snout to point at each of their hands before pointing to the door.

"I think he wants us to try opening the door together," Lachlan said.

She huffed, but she placed her hand atop the knob. Next, Lachlan's hand came down over hers, wrapping her in warmth. Heat radiated up her fingers and spread through her body, like the cottage had just cranked the heat up by several degrees.

The moment they touched the door in unison, the lock clicked open, and the cool outside air rushed in to greet Eliza's hot face.

"I think the house likes us together," Lachlan laughed.

"Don't start that nonsense," Eliza warned. "Now, where exactly is the tree farm?"

Lachlan pulled out the Airbnb's brochure from his back pocket and waved it. He opened it, running a finger along the map. "X marks the spot."

They trudged up the hill and through the snow, the hush of the forest only broken by the crunch of their boots underfoot and the rhythmic creak of pine trees as the wind picked up.

Every meter or so, a fresh piece of bread appeared alongside the road—golden and steamy against the cold snow. Gretel had said that Hansel's breadcrumbs were of a "special sort," designed to keep wanderers from getting lost no matter the season, even in the thickest snowfall.

What Hansel hadn't accounted for was Puffcake's ability to put down.

Without fail, the little sugar sprite took his sweet time hopping down from Eliza's makeshift scarf sling to pause by each breadcrumb. Then, he'd gobble up the breadcrumb right there on the path.

"Puffcake!" Eliza called, "Those aren't for eating. We'll need them to find our way back to the cottage."

Puffcake shot her a defiant look, as if he wasn't one bit remorseful.

It was helpful that the blizzard had not seemed to touch the woods with the same kind of intensity as it had in the cottage. Even the trails were only lightly covered in snow, but still visible.

"Do you think that the cottage somehow created the blizzard to trap us inside together?" Eliza asked.

"Wouldn't surprise me," answered Lachlan.

Behind them, Puffcake flapped his wings hard as he struggled to keep up. His breath came out in little, quick puffs of flurries. Eliza stopped halfway up the incline, unwound her scarf, and gently cupped her hands. "Come here, you little over-baked spice bread."

Puffcake gave a satisfied purr as he settled himself into the scarf. Soon, he was fast asleep, snoring with every inhale.

Her mobile dinged. She frowned as she glanced at

the message. It was from an unknown number, but she knew exactly who sent it. Her stomach tightened.

Davis

> You bloody serious, Liz? You blocked me? Really mature. No wonder you lost the bakery. Couldn't handle the heat, could you?

Tears pricked at her eyes. He could be so mean sometimes. And he knew she hated it when he called her Liz.

"Everything okay?" asked Lachlan.

"Mhmm," she hummed, faking a smile. "Of course. Sorry, it's just . . Someone from back home. You can take the girl away from the bakery, but you can't take the bakery away from the girl."

Lachlan arched a brow, unconvinced by her deflection. "I thought you came here to escape for a little while."

"Thought so, too," Eliza mumbled. "Turns out you can't in a world full of toxic exes and mobile phones."

He shoved his hands in his pockets, slowing his pace just a little. "Maybe it'd be best to turn it off for a little while."

"Quite thick coming from you," she said. "How many villas have you closed on since you've been here?"

"Closed? Zero. Inquired? About four."

She just shot him a look as if to prove her point.

"It's the *holidays*," he defended, as if that was supposed to excuse the hypocrisy away. "I'd be an idiot not to at least answer emails this time of year. It's a goldmine. Besides, I *like* my work. It was my sister who told me to take a break, mind you."

He blew out a breath, the puff of air diffusing in the frigid air. "Although I admit, I tend to dive into it too heavily when things aren't going well, and she probably caught on to that. But it is fun for me, at least."

"Sometimes it feels good to just get off the grid for a bit. Doesn't it?" she nudged him. "These days, it's almost impossible. Anyone and everyone can reach out to you in an instant. Even if you don't want them to," she bit out the last bit. She fidgeted with her phone in her hand, just waiting for another string of hateful messages to roll in. Thankfully, they never came.

She deleted the message, pushing Davis from her mind as best she could.

She was so lost in her thoughts that she hadn't realized they reached the Christmas tree farm. String lights were hung between each aisle, and the branches were lightly dusted with fresh snow. Lachlan led them down every aisle, eyeing each one of them like he was shopping for a new vehicle. He kept saying things like, "Hmmm, too big."

"Too small."

"Eh, maybe."

At about the fifth aisle, Eliza huffed. "I thought I was choosing, anyway. And must you be so picky?"

"Yes," he answered, "I have to set my standards high or else I'll be begging for us to take back the ugliest one because I'll feel sorry for it."

"Well, don't make the other trees self-conscious in the process," Eliza said.

Lachlan said something about how there was *"a profound lesson somewhere in there,"* but she wasn't paying attention. She'd found it: the perfect tree. It stood just a little taller than Lachlan, about six and a half feet tall, its branches thick and bushy. It was the perfect storybook shape with a thick base sloping toward a skinny top.

"There," she pointed, interrupting Lachlan mid-sentence.

"Now *that's* a Christmas tree," Lachlan replied with a whistle, walking in a circle to inspect every side of it. "I knew you had good taste, Snow. I just knew it."

Suddenly, a tree behind Lachlan tilted over and dumped a cascade of snow on top of his head. He stood there, blinking, frost covering his dark eyelashes.

Eliza couldn't help but laugh. "That's not magic. That's just straight-up karma for insulting the other trees."

"Point taken." He hoisted the tree up onto his shoulder and carried it to the front. He handed the cashier one hundred and fifty pounds. "Merry Christmas," Lachlan said to him with a warm smile.

Eliza raised her brows, surprised. "Big spender."

"Guess all the overpriced open houses finally paid off," he said, the two of them setting off back in the direction they came to the cottage. Puffcake was still sound asleep in Eliza's scarf.

"Your job's really that lucrative, huh?"

"It is when you work as much as I do," he turned to her with a half-smile. "Because what else does a single man like me in his late twenties have to do besides sell to his secondary-school friends who are married with two kids and a goldendoodle?"

Eliza laughed, noting how he explicitly mentioned he was single. Piper was going to flip at the news. "I guess spend it on an overpriced Christmas tree."

"Exactly. This is my wild phase. Blow all my money on getting stuck in a gingerbread house with a beautiful woman and impress her with pine needles and too-small baking aprons."

She desperately tried not to smile and swallowed nervously. "Desperate times."

"You have no idea."

She silently slipped out her phone and quickly typed a message to Piper.

> Can confirm—single.

Before she could put it back in her pocket, the message was read, and the three little dots appeared, showing Piper was already typing.

Then the *shoomp* of a reply.

You're the luckiest girl in the world.

Chapter Ten

Gingerbread Crimes

Eliza and Lachlan entered the cottage the same way they came, their hands pressed against each other on the knob. The lock clicked its satisfaction, allowing them to pass through the threshold.

Inside, the house enveloped Eliza in warmth, clove, and cinnamon. It felt like she'd curled up inside an overly large hearth. Lachlan placed the tree in the corner beside the hearth, just where Isadora had been decorating the tree in her memory. At last, he stepped back with his hands on his hips to admire the placement. His gaze drifted to the sofa across the room, and he tilted his head. Eliza followed his line of sight.

Sitting on top of the velvet cushions were several containers, like a pile of wrapped presents waiting to be opened. A single red ornament fell onto the floor and landed with a soft clink next to Lachlan's foot.

"I think the house wants us to decorate it," he said.

The house's fire snapped and crackled in response, casting shadows along the walls.

The boxes held several vintage ornaments, fresh home-made strings of oranges, glittering lights, and spools of expensive ribbon.

"I feel like we're being watched," Lachlan said, coming to Eliza's side.

"We are," corrected Eliza as she held up a Sugar Plum Fairy ornament. "You'd better be on your best behavior or else the house may hide your beloved sock collection."

"Just not the ones with bells," he said a little louder so the house would hear.

She handed him the ballerina ornament. "Start hanging. I'm trusting you not to mess up the aesthetic."

"We're going for an aesthetic, are we?"

"Always."

He adjusted the lights, hanging them too far away from each other. "How's this?"

"Absolutely not." She came over to adjust his work. "There. Better."

"That's what you get for trusting me," he said.

They fell into a rhythm, handing off the spool of string lights as they carefully hung them inside the tree.

From the corner of her eye, she saw Lachlan glance at her. All of a sudden, she felt like she didn't know what to do with her hands.

"So, Snow," he began. "What do you like to do with your free time? You know, other than baking and booking week-long gingerbread escapades?"

She continued, carefully placing the lights on the tree, thinking. "Well, there's this little pub a few streets away from my flat. There's a trivia night there every Thursday. Sounds so silly when I say it out loud."

"Silly? What for?" he asked, seeming genuinely curious.

She scrunched her nose. "I don't know. I guess not everyone is into those types of things. My ex wasn't, at least."

Lachlan huffed out a laugh, though it sounded anything but amused. "Not his idea of fun, is it? Pint in hand, pub quiz going, and the rugby game humming along in the background … Honestly, does this bloke enjoy living?"

Eliza rolled her eyes, passing off the string of lights his way. She hadn't meant for this to take yet another Davis turn. So she steered the other way. "I also like to cycle. Well, spin classes. You know, where you go into a dark room that blares loud music. It's basically like clubbing on a stationary bike."

"No wonder your legs are so toned," he said, rounding the tree to place the lights on the next set of branches. "Figured it must be from all the standing you do in the kitchen."

Eliza blushed, thankful he was busy around the other side of the tree so he couldn't see her face. She hadn't realized he was paying attention. "Wait a minute. Were you checking me out?"

He poked his head out from the side of the tree. "Observing, admiring, checking out ... It's all the same, really."

With another eye-roll, she thrust out her hand for the Christmas lights. He handed them over, their fingertips brushing ever-so-slightly. "What do *you* like to do? You know, other than selling overpriced beach houses on the coast and admiring a stranger's legs?"

"Plenty of things, Snow. Admiring your legs is a recent hobby of mine that I take very seriously, thank you very much."

She shoved him, muttering, "Creep," but she couldn't stop the blush that continued to spread up her neck and into her cheeks.

"Used to play rugby with my mates," Lachlan started. "I played for the University of Southampton until I got injured. Tore my ACL."

She looked from Lachlan to the tree, swallowing hard. She didn't know what to say, so she said the only thing she knew how to. "I'm sorry to hear that."

"Don't be," he said, taking the lights from her, their hands brushing. "Everything happens for a reason." His eyes locked on hers. "And for the record? You're not a stranger. I've been living with you for the past day, and I very much like getting to know you."

Eliza misstepped and accidentally bumped into Lachlan as she was handing the loop of lights to him to hang around the back.

"Careful," he warned, grabbing her waist to steady her.

"Your fault!" she joked, her face practically burning alive. It felt like someone had stuck her directly over the fire to roast. "You were blocking all the light."

He looked down just as she looked up, and for the time being, the world stood still. Her gaze locked on his deepest brown eyes of molten chocolate; only the kind you'd find in the finest of bakeries.

"Um," he cleared his throat. His gaze softened. "You have glitter on your bottom lip."

"Do I?" Eliza breathed. Her heart was stuck somewhere between her throat and her stomach.

"Uh huh."

Slowly, he reached up, brushing his thumb across her lower lip to wipe away the speck. But then his hand stilled. Her breathing hitched, caught in the silence stuck between them. All she could feel was the warmth of his skin pressed on her face. And for a breath, he held her there, the world narrowing down to their single point of contact.

She stood frozen as the icicles hung outside the cottage. She was suddenly too aware of everything. The way her breath quickened, her heart racing beneath her ribs, the comforting scent of evergreen that clung to his skin.

Her heart pounded so fast that she was sure Lachlan could feel it.

Something shifted along the rafters above them. There was a rustling sound, like frosting was being swirled over a cake. Emerald vines of piping curled down from the ceiling, rapidly lacing themselves as it descended—no, *grew*— to meet them. In the center, just over Lachlan and Eliza's heads, was a sprig of mistletoe.

"I swear this house has no chill," Eliza nervously laughed.

"Neither do I, apparently." Lachlan lifted her chin with his thumb, silently waiting for the cue.

Was it the magic of the house, the nostalgia of the holiday, or something else entirely that made Lachlan seem so drawn to her? Eliza couldn't tell. But the question haunted her: would he one day wake up and treat her like something he'd grown tired of? Was he even thinking about the future, or just living in the magical moments shared within these warm, ginger-bread walls?

And how long would the chemistry spark before the flame burned out? When was it a matter of time before his love, or infatuation, or whatever this was, quietly faded, too, vanishing before it was ever even truly hers?

She took a step back. "I'm not kissing you simply because a sentient gingerbread Airbnb encourages me to."

Puffcake let out a massive, melodramatic yawn from his luxurious mixing bowl bed.

"What if it wasn't encouraging you to do so? Would you have a change of heart?" He asked.

Eliza shrugged. "I would—"

Lachlan flashed Eliza a smile. "So you *would* kiss me?"

"I wasn't finished!" she floundered, swatting at him. "Enough with your antics."

"Hey, I'm just an innocent bystander." Lachlan put his hands up. "I'm just as much a victim to these gingerbread crimes as you are."

The mistletoe shook from side to side, as if in anticipation of the big moment. But it never came.

Eliza pushed him away playfully. "Sure you are, Casanova."

He caught her hand and held it there, just above his heart. She felt the soft thump-thump of his pulse beating like a steady drum. She wondered if he could feel hers through the shallow veins of her wrist. And if she'd thought her heart was beating fast earlier, now it was about to sputter out of control.

"It's good you don't give in to peer pressure, Snow." His expression grew serious, his eyes meeting hers once more and drowning her in chocolatey goodness. "I want *you* to want to kiss me. Not because the gingerbread house says so." He said with a wink.

Eliza nervously stepped around Lachlan, and he

broke his grip, but the feeling of his hand on hers still lingered. "C'mon," she said, gasping for air. "Let's finish this tree before it tangles us up together in tinsel."

Chapter Eleven

Raspberry Creams,
a Letter, and a Dream

Soon, the tree was shimmering with glitter, lights, and pure magic. Even Puffcake was impressed.

It was well past midnight now, and Eliza just pulled her second batch of chocolate chip biscuits out of the oven. After she and Lachlan set up the tree, the mistletoe had vanished as quickly as it had gotten there, disappearing from the ceiling with a *pop* before bursting into a cloud of sparkles.

If it weren't for the sparkles left over on the mahogany rug, Eliza would've thought she imagined the whole encounter.

Lachlan had stayed in the kitchen with her, mostly

because the gingerbread house made him. This time, however, it was kind enough to allow Lachlan to use his laptop.

They worked in silence, but Eliza felt his eyes on her. It made her more clumsy than usual.

She became acutely aware of how she moved, and what kind of expressions she made while she measured and whisked and poured. His comment earlier about her legs had created a deeper sort of complex within her than it needed to be, but she still couldn't seem to get it —*or him*—out of her head.

He watched Eliza across the island, her blonde hair tied back, brows furrowed as she shifted flour into a chilled bowl. She stopped mid-sprinkle to cut her eyes at him. "Is there a problem?" she asked.

"Not at all," Lachlan said back. His expression softened. "It's just, you look so much more grown-up when you bake."

She lifted a brow, still trying to concentrate on the task at hand. "Are you calling me a gran-gran?"

"No!" he backtracked. "It—isn't a bad thing. You just look wise and … timeless."

"Timeless?" she repeated.

Lachlan shrugged. "The opposite of old." Then, he reached up and brushed a strand of blonde hair away from her eyebrow. "Stunning, actually."

"Hmmm," she thought, not entirely sure how to respond. Her hands shook at his comment. "Well, be careful with your words next time, or else I might start demanding you call me 'nana.' And this doesn't get you out of doing the dishes tonight, even if it was a good attempt."

"What was your nan like?" he asked.

Eliza paused her mixing for a fraction, wooden spoon hovering mid-air. The question caught her off guard. Not because she felt like he was prying, but because she felt like it was rare. No one asked about Nan anymore. None of her hometown acquaintances, her ex, or even her own mother, brought it up to her for fear she might snap on them and start crying.

It wasn't right, but no one knew how to properly grieve with her. She realized, throughout her nan's treatment, that the world preferred silence. As if pretending the loss didn't exist and somehow made it easy to carry.

Eliza wasn't like that. She could never be like that.

"She was wonderful," Eliza's words spilled out more in a whisper of a confession. Her throat tightened at the thought of her. She closed her eyes, and for a moment, she could almost picture it: her nan, standing right here beside her, apron tied crookedly and humming along to some tune on the record player.

Eliza's voice trembled as she spoke. "If she'd been here, she'd be standing in this cottage, in this very kitchen, whipping up truffles and little sweet treats to tuck in each of our stockings." She gave a soft, wistful laugh. "She used to do that each year. Everyone always had at least one thing that was different from all the rest. My dad always got orange peels dipped in white chocolate because he swore it was 'healthier,'" Eliza air-quoted.

"And I would always get raspberry creams because I always tried sneaking those when I thought she wasn't looking."

He smiled, leaning in a little closer. "She sounds lovely."

"She was." She stared into the mixing bowl. Her eyes glimmered with fresh tears. "She made the holiday feel enchanting, in a way. I still marvel at the magic of this place, but I know the real magic of the season was always her."

"You miss her." There wasn't room for questioning in his voice.

Eliza just nodded several times, her throating bobbing. "Every day." She wiped a tear. "But when I'm baking, it feels like she's right *here*. Watching. Maybe even helping."

"I think she'd be proud."

Eliza met his eyes. "Thank you," she choked out. She went back to stirring, as if she repeated the circular motion in the batter enough times, she might be able to summon her nan's laughter just to hear it again. "I hope so."

Lachlan stretched a yawn as he looked at the clock. One thirty in the morning. He shut his laptop. "Snow, I'm going to have to call it for tonight."

Eliza laughed, "Well, you'd better hurry now before the cottage barricades you in here again with me. I'm afraid there isn't a large enough mixing bowl for you to bum like Puffcake."

As if on cue, Puffcake let out a snore from inside his copper sleeping chamber.

"Oh, I wasn't in here tonight because I had to be," Lachlan said. The truth hung in the air between them, thick as whipping cream. "By the by, I think you're going to smash this baking contest. You should get some rest, too, instead of stressing about it."

"You sound like my mum," she shook her head. "I have one more recipe in mind, and then I'll retire."

He stuck out his pinky finger. "Promise?"

"Promise." She interlocked her pinky with his. "Goodnight." She gave a half-hearted parting, and was surprised when the kitchen let him exit. Granted, the living room was only about twenty feet away, but Eliza had a suspicion it had something to do with Lachlan's confession—and what she held in her hands now.

Eliza eagerly opened *Isadora's Memory Baking Cookbook* and flipped to the next page, where the recipe, *Silent Night Soufflé*, was.

She read off the ingredients: eggs, milk, cream, sugar.

They sounded promising enough, but the steps were more fragmented than usual, like Isadora had jotted the notes down quickly. Even the handwriting was scratchy and uneven, and the words looked like they were formed from a shaky hand. It wasn't like her usual, romantic font.

Still, Eliza got to baking, trusting the house. She cracked two eggs, folded in the sugar and dairy products … She noted that there wasn't any sort of spell like the recipes before, and the batter didn't shine like the others. Instead, it was dull and gray, despite the yellow yolks that should've made the custard appear a pleasant cream.

She did as the rest of the instructions insisted, preparing and baking the entire time in complete silence. She preheated the oven to 180 degrees Celsius, baked the dessert for thirty minutes, and set it out to cool for ten minutes.

Immediately upon taking the first bite, she was transported. She stood near the hearth, the fire weak and dim inside. The record player wasn't playing anything, and the lights from the tree that once glistened in the corner weren't even plugged in.

In the kitchen stood Isadora, alone. She was hunched over a bowl of batter, her once bright smile now bleak. The air smelled of burnt sugar, scorched biscuits, and crushed dreams.

Thick smoke rolled from the oven. Isadora opened it, the trembling of her hands even apparent through the oven mitts. Tears swam in her eyes, her makeup streaking down her face.

There was no husband. No laughter. No hands to sweep her off her feet.

Just a letter signed off by Ernest's name at the end.

Isadora,

I'm not quite sure how to do this other than to just come out and say it. I believe it's time for me to move on. When I married you, I didn't expect you to be like this. I thought that maybe we simply were unlucky in our efforts, but now I know that it will never happen because you simply cannot. I only wish you'd told me sooner. You only baked to keep your heart at bay, but baking doesn't fix everything. I've met someone. Please know that I didn't want this. I never wanted this. I only wanted to start a family.

Sincerely,

Ernest

The dessert was black around the edges, charred and dry. She watched it cool with dull eyes, but didn't try to eat it. She reread the letter several times, the look of utter devastation marring her beautiful features. Then, Isadora collapsed on the kitchen floor, buried her face in her hands, and wept.

The scene faded away, and Eliza was swept back in the present, the same kitchen swelling with the scent of vanilla and spices. But the scorched notes of Isadora's memory still bled into the present.

Eliza stepped away from the counter, her heart aching.

The recipe book was no longer showing her sweet beginnings—it was showing their burnt and bitter ending.

And all Eliza could ask herself was *why*. Why would it show Isadora's joy only for it to end in such heartbreak? Why would it show these memories if there wasn't something she was supposed to change about them? But *what* was she supposed to change about them? This was eighty years ago.

Eliza pressed her palms into the counter. The magic tonight didn't feel light and whimsical anymore. It felt heavy and full of sorrow, like even the cottage remembered the night of Isadora's heartbreak, and it'd slipped back into that solemn quiet, too.

To take her mind off the tragic scenario, Eliza quickly whipped together a batch of sugar biscuits. She popped them in the oven, her mind still tangled up in the memory

Was the house playing some cruel joke on her? Or did the house know that Eliza knew pain like this all too well? That no matter how sweet the love may be at the start, it always has the potential to burn you? She still smelled the lingering scent of charred dessert, a ghost of Isadora's grief. She suddenly felt cold despite the fire roaring over in the hearth.

When she checked on her chocolate chip biscuits, her eyes widened. "*Biscuits,*" she muttered under her breath. She'd burnt them.

She gawked at the biscuits, bewildered. They hadn't

even been in there longer than *five minutes*. How could they have possibly burned?

Before she could make sense of it, Puffcake let out a choking noise, startling Eliza. Tiny clouds of white sugar burst from his nostrils.

"Shhh!" Eliza hissed, rushing over to him. She placed a finger over his tiny, frosted snout, "Don't you *dare* wake up Lachlan, or else I'll never hear the end of it."

Puffcake paused his coughing spell and narrowed his gumdrop eyes at her.

"I'll remove my finger when you're done with your theatrics," she said.

He simply stayed quiet.

Satisfied that the crisis was contained (other than the terrible smell), she sighed, relaxing a little. That was enough baking for one evening.

She yawned and headed for the stairs. Puffcake fluttered behind her, wings drooping in shared exhaustion. Upstairs, she settled herself down in the bed and wrapped the blanket around her like a cinnamon roll. She sank into the mattress as Puffcake settled himself beside her on the pillow next to her head. He let out one final breath, dusting the sheets with a fine layer of powdered sugar.

That night, she dreamt of mistletoe and twinkling lights. Of pie, evergreen-infused air, and laughter. Of someone softly humming Christmas carols in the kitchen, wearing a too-small apron. He twirled her around and around in a red gingham dress that wasn't hers, flour clinging to her rosy cheeks.

Then, his hands suddenly let go of her. She was spinning out of control. She slammed into the kitchen cabinets, banging her elbow hard on the countertop.

A voice called out to her, and she turned to find no one was there. The room had grown cold. Quiet and stale, like a picture gone wrong and fading out of focus.

A bag of flour thudded to the floor, sending Eliza's heart hammering. The powdery substance caked where Eliza stepped, leaving a trail of footprints behind. Laced within the flour was the familiar cursive penmanship Eliza knew too well. The same handwriting from the cookbook.

Let love not last here if mine cannot.

Chapter Twelve

Baking Alone

Eliza blinked awake to find Puffcake still asleep beside her. He was upside down on his back. For a creature the size of a ferret, he snored like a lawn-mower. She stifled a laugh and snapped a picture to show Lachlan before she quietly slipped out of bed. Pulling on her thickest socks and comfiest clothes, she tiptoed her way down the stairs, the warmth of the cottage embracing her like a memory.

Eliza moved to the kitchen with a renewed sense of energy. Morning light spilled across the golden counter-tops, illuminating the copper alliances. *Isadora's*

Memory Baking Cookbook was already on the counter, as if it had been waiting for her. Expectant.

She was sure she put it back up last night.

She didn't open it, nor did she crack open the tin of recipe cards on the baker's rack.

She wanted this to be her victory, not someone else's. Not just a copycat recipe from Isadora. Still, the presence of the book oddly grounded her. It felt like the women who'd baked before her in this cottage were cheering her on as she carried the baton of their legacy. Baking was an eternal art, and she was keeping the wonderful tradition alive.

Eliza pulled out the cranberries and oranges, set them in a mixing bowl, and got to work. She zested the citrus and mashed the cranberries, red staining her fingertips as she added whipping cream to a large mixing bowl. She mixed and measured and poured until she was proud of the consistency. Soon, zest and holiday spices filled the air.

She thought of Isadora's words laced along the gingerbread floor last night. The dream felt more real, like another memory, only this time it had found Eliza in her sleep. She couldn't make sense of it. She felt like the house was trying to communicate something to her …

Gretel mentioned that the cottage only became enchanted when couples stayed here. Was it enchanted *because* of Isadora? Was the cottage showing Isadora's heartbreak to warn her?

She hadn't noticed when, but at some point, Puffcake came paddling down the stairs, blinking through his hazy, lavender eyes. He lapped at the extra batter she'd dropped on the floor. "Helping clean up my messes?" She chuckled at him, scratching behind his ear.

Her hands moved gingerly, pouring cream and sugar. A drawer slid open for her, revealing a bundle of cinnamon sticks she'd forgotten to add. A whisk hovered in mid-air, and she grabbed it.

"Thank you," she said to the house. She swore the flames in the hearth responded with a spark.

Christmas carols crackled from the record player in the corner, and the electric mixer churned in time with the beat. The spice rack spun on its own as she reached for cloves. The cottage was alive, and today it was her baking partner.

She hummed quietly as she worked, sweet contentedness at last.

Come to think of it, the cottage was *unusually* quiet. She padded onto the patio, expecting Lachlan to be nursing a cup of steaming coffee, but the space was empty. Maybe he was in the shower, she reasoned, but the door was propped open, the light off, and no steam wafting between the cracks. No sign of him.

His boots and winter coat were nowhere to be found, but his bag still lay beside the Christmas tree. Had he left in such a hurry that he'd forgotten it? Or worse, had he not even cared to take it?

She glanced around again, sure that she was mistaken, but there was no trail of footprints across the flour-coated floor. No creaking floors. No one was teasing her about her sleep-tangled hair.

Then it hit her. She was truly alone in the house. He'd gone outside *without* her.

Had he taken the first opportunity to split when the cottage would let him? She denied the heaviness in her gut, excusing it as hunger pangs. Did she say something wrong last night? Had she shared too much of her sadness about losing her nan? Regret and embarrassment filled her as something sharp spiked within her chest.

She thought of Isadora, of Silent Night Soufflé. Was this the cottage's way of saying they weren't right for each other? Was this *Lachlan's* way of saying they weren't right for each other?

Not that *she* hoped they were right for each other.

Was this how it ended? Not with a slamming door and yelling choice words, like with Davis, but with silence. With so many unspoken words and left out feelings—just as it'd been for Isadora.

And it was Isadora's chant that rattled around in her mind: *Let love not last here if mine cannot.* But who was Eliza kidding? It'd ended before it ever really began, and it certainly hadn't been love.

Still, her steps were hurried as she crossed the cottage, eagerly parting the sugar-laced curtains. His rental Land Rover was still there, parked in the same spot it had been since he'd arrived.

She blinked, relieved but still confused. Then she

smiled to herself, thinking of her friend Piper. This would be what her friend called the "romantic plot twist."

Maybe he had gone into the forest to get more firewood, or was on a call to negotiate with one of his clients about a house. Maybe it wasn't that deep, after all. But she didn't check.

If Lachlan wanted to tell her where he was, he would've told her. He would've left a note, sent a text. There were at least five different ways he could have communicated to her, *"Hey, I'm stepping out,"* but he didn't.

It dawned on her then that he didn't have her phone number. But still, a note would have sufficed. She told herself not to be upset about it, but the sting lingered. Like a paper cut that you didn't know was there until it stung when you washed your hands.

Fine. Let him be mysterious. She had scones to bake and a competition to win.

Though with Lachlan gone, she thought better of it. Curiosity tugged at her. She thought of Isadora and the odd dream she'd had last night. Had it all been a coincidence, especially now that Lachlan was nowhere to be found?

She practically sprinted over to Isadora's cookbook, eager to find what the next recipe might reveal about this enigmatic woman. She'd been unable to bake these recipes until late in the evening once Lachlan was asleep, but now she was free to do it in broad daylight.

Once Lachlan returned—if he planned on doing so —Eliza would throw the recipe out and claim that it wasn't any good. She still wasn't ready to tell him the truth about her findings. It still felt oddly too personal to share with anyone just yet, and now that she'd come this far, she was invested. She needed answers.

There was something about Isadora's story that felt connected to this house and the strange events that happened here. Maybe this book of memories was even the key to why the cottage only trapped couples here and no one else.

Her phone buzzed in the band of her leggings. With sticky fingers, she pulled it free. Piper.

How's Mr. Perfectly Fine?

Eliza couldn't help but chuckle.

Gone.

Was all she sent back.

She locked her phone and set it face down on the counter. Her phone instantly buzzed, but she ignored it all and set off to work.

She flipped to the next page, and her heart sank at the name of the dish. *Barren Cradle Bake*. Next to the title, there was a date, six months before the date that Eliza had read in the newspaper, Ernest had been reading the cottage.

Eliza preheated the oven to 190 degrees, and quickly pulled the ingredients: Strawberry jam, sugar, eggs, and vanilla. Eliza didn't allow any time for the cake to cool before plunging in a spoon and tasting, the clouds of the memory parting for her like a veil.

There stood Isadora, clutching her belly as she entered the room. It wasn't the warm, lively kitchen Eliza knew so well, but another she hadn't seen before. It was quieter, sweeter, and unfamiliar. A crib sat in the corner, spun from delicate isomalt and embellished with candied rose petals.

Then Isadora fell to her knees, broken and sobbing. And in that instant, Eliza understood. The name of the recipe, and why she was here. This was a memory within a memory, a step further back in time to fill the spaces between the story. This wasn't a happy memory. It was six months before the others.

Isadora wasn't pregnant anymore.

It was just as Eliza had cleaned up the kitchen and tossed the rest of the Barren Cradle Cake out, when she heard the bells in the front door jingle. Her heart leapt as cold air came rushing in. She turned to see Lachlan standing there, stomping the snow off his boots by the door.

In his arms, there was a bundle of brown wrapping paper, a sprig of rosemary tied around it with velvet ribbon. All of Eliza's questions about how he managed to leave died on her tongue. Instead, she crossed her arms, brow raised. "What is *that*?"

His eyes sparkled as he handed it to her. "Open it."

She eyed him wearily, untying the string and ripping apart the paper. In it was a rolling pin, carved from real wood and looking several years old. Despite its age, it was in mint condition.

Eliza seemed to be at a loss for words. She just stared down at it.

When she said nothing, he said, "You probably have a million of these already." He gave an apologetic smile. "But I saw it yesterday as we passed by that old charity shop. I pleaded with the house for an hour this morning to go without you to surprise you with it. At first, it didn't believe me, so it kept pelting snow at me along the road just to make sure I remembered the path."

"That's really thoughtful of you." She wasn't sure how to take his generosity. It definitely didn't have to be some sort of romantic gesture. Maybe he was just being friendly. It was the season of giving, after all.

A smile grew on his lips, satisfied. "Don't assume my intentions were one hundred percent pure, Snow. I'll be expecting something hot and sweet in return."

Eliza's cheeks flared crimson.

"Obviously, I meant in baked goods," Lachlan added.

"Lucky for you, I was just about to get started on the first batch of desserts for the contest," she smiled. She didn't dare comment on how she had to pitch the first set because she'd let them set out too long while she had a little baking sidequest.

"I decided to make scones. I thought I'd name them Winter Hearth for their warmth and Christmas nostalgia. What do you think?"

His eyes lit up, matching her excitement. "I think that's brilliant."

"Good," she said over her shoulder, already prepping for her next bake. "You can be my taste judge."

"I'm honored," he said, placing his hand dramatically to his chest. "You better have brought your A-game, Snow. I'm as picky about my sweets as I am about the houses I sell."

"High standards, hm? You're wearing the same flannel from two days ago," she teased.

"I have the highest standards." He looked at her, more intently now. "About the things that matter in life. Like scones and vintage rolling pins."

Before she could say anything else, her phone buzzed again, reminding her of the several she received earlier. She finally checked them. They were all from Piper.

WHAT

> oh God, we're reaching the climax of the Hallmark movie. What did you fight about?

> what did you say to make him leave?

> are the cultural differences between the city slicker and the country boy too great?!

Eliza groaned, shaking her head. She set her phone down on the island just as the oven dinged. She pulled on the oven mitts to get the scones out. Another message buzzed.

Behind her, she heard Lachlan laugh. She turned, seeing him over the top of her phone. Lachlan looked shamelessly guilty, and Eliza raised a brow, color filling her cheeks. "Did you just read my texts?"

He held his hands up in innocence. "In my defense, it was literally right in front of me. It's not like I grabbed it, unlocked it, and read."

What did Piper say this time?

Eliza crossed the kitchen and snatched her phone. After double-tapping the screen, she read:

> FR though… where did he go

Eliza sighed, partially relieved. Not that she wanted him to read any of her texts, especially between her and Piper. But if her privacy was going to be breached, she was glad it was the one he read.

He raised a brow, smugly leaning against the counter. "Does this mean that someone was concerned for me?"

Eliza ignored him and silently went to her iPhone settings and disabled her message previews. "There," she muttered, tossing her phone down again. "Now your nosy self can mind your own business."

Lachlan looked far too amused. "Are you at least going to reply? Tell her that I came back in one piece?"

"No, because I wasn't talking about *you*."

"Oh, really? Who were you talking about then?" His voice lifted in skepticism.

"My ... cat," she said, a beat too late.

"Your cat," he repeated.

She nodded, doubling down. "Yeah. My friend lost him this morning."

"What's your cat's name?"

"Fluffy." She blurted out the first thing she could think of.

Puffcake and Lachlan exchanged a knowing look. "Creative," he muttered.

"But, to be fair, you could've left a note."

"So you *were* worried for me?"

"All things considered, yes. With my cat missing, and the house being what it is, I couldn't help but worry."

"Then," he got out his phone from his coat pocket and slid it across the counter to Eliza. "We should exchange numbers. To soothe your anxiety, of course."

"Of course," she said. She punched in her number and added her name. "Eliza Jane Snow."

Her phone dinged a second later. She glanced down at the screen, and his contact photo appeared. It was a picture of him on the cliffside of the coast, his arm slung around a German Shepherd.

"Who's the dog?"

"My Fluffy."

She snorted and tossed him a scone in response. He caught it with one hand, set it down on the island, and inspected it at all angles like a gemstone under appraisal. "Eight out of ten for presentation."

"I didn't know I was being judged on presentation!" she croaked.

"Well, you will be, tomorrow, " he quipped. "Might as well start early. You'd better straighten up, Snow, or tomorrow won't go in your favor."

She rolled her eyes, placing a hand on her hip. "Shut up and taste the bloody thing."

He obeyed, took a bite, and his eyes grew wide. "This is ..." he licked his lips. "Amazing."

He paused, chewing thoughtfully. "*But* I think it could need something else. A little extra *'Christmas pizzazz.'* I mean, don't get me wrong, it truly is amazing. But I've tasted better from you, Snow."

Eliza tasted one herself. She couldn't say she disagreed.

It was good, but it wasn't glowing. It wasn't like all the other recipes that floated toward her on a whim.

"You think it needs a dash more zest?" she asked.

Puffcake nodded vigorously, twitching his tail. Lachlan only shrugged. "I'm not here to tell the master baker what to do. Only to judge." He held his hands up in surrender. "But dang, your exes must've put on a fair few stone after dating you. You're bloody dangerous."

Warmth burned Eliza's cheeks, and she wasn't sure if it was from flattery or embarrassment.

He quickly backpedaled. "I didn't mean to ... I just meant you're really talented." For the first time this week, Lachlan looked embarrassed.

"It's fine." Eliza smiled dryly. "I know you didn't mean anything by it. Just be careful what you say. Or else next time I'll feed you a burnt scone."

She texted her friend back, figuring she'd waited long enough.

False Alarm. He came back.

For some reason, that made Eliza ridiculously happy.

Chapter Thirteen

Winter Hearth

As the day went on, it seemed like Lachlan, Eliza, and Puffcake had settled into a pretty easy routine. Lachlan tapped away briskly at emails between sips of hot chocolate, the glow of the screen reflecting in his mug. Across the counter, Eliza folded the dough for her second round of scones.

This batch carried its own twist, slight tweaks from yesterday's recipe. Extra flakes of citrus zest wove throughout the dough like confetti, promising a burst of freshness to balance out the bite of the cranberry and the savory of the butter.

To drive the flavor home further, she decided to

forsake chopped almonds altogether. Their heaviness only seemed to weigh down the dough before. Instead, she added almond extract, a concentrated liquid that wrapped warmth and sweetness around the cottage's kitchen like a large blanket.

The room had settled into a gentle rhythm of small noises: the steady clack of keys as Lachlan typed, the occasional *clink* of a measuring spoon against a bowl, and the faint hum of Puffcake's snores as he lost himself in sugary dreams. Beneath it all was the muffled crackle of holiday tunes floating in the air from the record player.

Lachlan let out a huff, breaking their long stretch of silence. "Do you ever get tired of listening to the same Christmas music? It's been going on for five hours now."

Eliza shot him a glare. "Do *you* ever get tired of working?" she asked, but she already knew the answer.

He didn't look up from his screen. "There's always someone who needs answering."

"It's three days before Christmas," she said, wiping her hands on a towel. "The only replies you're going to get back are from the Grinch."

"Or from an insanely gorgeous beach house off Southampton," he said, flipping the laptop around for Eliza to see. He cracked his knuckles. "Enough commission off this bad boy to supply a lifetime of rolling pins."

Eliza's eyes widened. "Whoa. That *is* insanely

gorgeous." She flipped through all the pictures of the beach house, noting the scenic view, the six bedrooms, and the price. Lachlan must do very well for himself. "Impressive. Carry on." She slid it back around to him.

As if on cue, Puffcake fluttered over to the keyboard and stretched out across it like a cat. Lachlan swatted him away while Eliza laughed.

"He got icing all over my keys," Lachlan muttered.

"You can't win an argument against Puffcake. He lives for drama." She braced herself against the counter with both of her wrists, throwing the hand towel over her shoulder. She studied Lachlan for a moment, unsure exactly how to proceed. "I thought your sister sent you here on a getaway mission to *save* you from your work. Not just set aside more time to dive headlong into it."

He looked up at Eliza, meeting her gaze. He was contemplating something, only Eliza wasn't sure what until he closed his laptop softly and leaned back in his chair. "This is the first Christmas without my dad." His voice came low, cracking a little at the last word.

Eliza set down the bowl of sugar, momentarily abandoning her work. She said nothing in response, only silently waited for more, if he was willing to offer.

"He's still alive. Just with his new girlfriend on the Amalfi Coast. She was his secretary." He gave a tight smile, drumming his fingers on the island nervously. "Mum's visiting my sister in Brighton. I didn't want to intrude. They never invited me, and I never asked. And honestly, I didn't know if I could handle the whole *matching-jim-jams-and-pretend-we're-fine* family thing this year."

Eliza met his gaze, her heart twisting. "So you came here."

"So I came here," he nodded. "I needed a break, and as far away as I could get. My sister knew that. Guess she didn't read the fine print when she booked." He rubbed the back of his neck, "And I guess I didn't expect all this." He waved his hand through the air.

Eliza raised her brow. "What? You didn't expect a magical snowstorm, a feisty fire-breathing shortbread, or an antisocial baker? It was all in the fine print, Hollis."

He let out a laugh, flexing a little in his seat. "Especially the baker." His brown eyes locked on hers too long.

Puffcake snorted and batted his wings over to the hearth, clearly uncomfortable by the serious turn of conversation.

Eliza's chest swelled with a feeling she couldn't quite place. Was it pride? Satisfaction? "Well ... I'm glad you're here," she smiled genuinely.

"Me too."

"You're lucky I like you, or else you'd be confined to the living room—magical house rules or not," she said, pushing the bowl of coarse sugar across the table to him. Their fingers brushed in the transfer. "Here, help me with topping off the scones."

He grinned, already dusting the sugar onto the tops

of the desserts. "And miss out on the opportunity to be your trustee Sous-Chef? That would be tragic."

She took the pan of scones from the oven and bumped the door shut with her hip. "Well, if you're going to stick around, you might as well make yourself useful."

"Today's my first day besides burning a frozen pizza and making a mediocre breakfast. Now you're trusting me with a job so delicate?"

"Oh, hush. You're sprinkling sugar on top of the pastries, not disabling an atomic bomb."

"Okay, says the girl who bakes like it's an Olympic sport," Lachlan said behind his shoulder. "I'd better get half the spoil tomorrow for helping you out. How much is the contest for, anyway?"

"Five thousand pounds."

Lachlan whistled. "That's like a month's supply of flour and sugar for you, Snow."

"Yeah, or a down payment on a bakery."

Their shoulders brushed as she came next to him and began whipping up another batch.

"Is that really what you're going to spend the money on?" he asked.

Eliza immediately felt childish. She'd already failed once. What was Lachlan going to say to make her change her mind? It was probably foolish to try again, but she'd never know unless she did. She was never much of a risk-taker, but Gretel had already entered her in the contest. All she could do now was give it her all and aim for first place.

"Yes," she nodded once.

He stole a sideways glance at her, a smile tugging at his lip. "Think you'll smoke, Mrs. Elle Toe?"

"I'm certainly going to try."

"If you need help finding a place..." he nudged her playfully on the shoulder. "... I just so happen to know a charming realtor."

Eliza froze for a second, her hand buried deep in a bag of flour. Lachlan's words caught her off guard. Sure, he was being playful, but she heard the sincerity behind them. Help. Lachlan wanted to help her. "Oh? Is he cute?"

"Devastating." He smirked, "And the word's out that he's got a soft spot for sassy blondes who bake like their life depends on it."

Eliza snorted, feeling her face warm. "That's a very specific type."

Lachlan flashed his white teeth, abandoning his work to turn to her. He looked down, his smile almost blinding. "Turns out, it's my favorite."

Her fingers suddenly felt foreign and tingly, like she was having an out-of-body experience. Him flirting with her made her knees way more wobbly than it had any right to do. Why was a twenty-five year old woman *this* nervous over something so simple?

She still couldn't quite fathom why he would offer his help outside the safety of this holiday escape. It hinted at something more—something that connected them outside of the realm of this cottage's strange and mysterious enchantment. Something real that might follow them back from the world of make-believe that was this kitchen.

She wiped her hands off on her apron, nervously turning to face him. She took a deep breath, suddenly feeling the weight of everything unspoken between them. Whatever this was—whatever he was playing at ... It wouldn't last. She knew it.

They'd leave the day after Christmas, go their separate ways, and Lachlan would forget all about her. Chalk up the whole story to some weird coincidence.

"I had a bakery once," she blurted, not meeting his eyes. As soon as she said the words, she instantly wanted to take them back.

"Tell me about it."

She looked down, focusing her attention on where the lumps of dough sat on the flour-sprinkled countertop. "It was small. Nothing fancy. Just a bright blue building with white trim. A couple of employees to work the checkout. A door that jammed in the summer..." her voice grew into a whisper. "I poured everything into that place. My time, my money, every ounce of who I was.

"My fiancé—*ex*-fiancé—" she clarified, "co-signed the lease for me. He knew Honeycomb was everything to me, and he took it when we split. In the papers, he made it so that he owned fifty-one percent, so he owned the majority. I didn't have the money to fight him."

She gave a sad smile, remembering all of the drama again, her anger rekindling. Lachlan didn't offer to speak. Just offered his quiet presence next to her.

She laughed bitterly. "Which is funny because he always told me that baking was a silly career. That while I was busy playing housewife, he was out there making '*big boy money*.'"

Lachlan took a step forward, but didn't reach out to touch her. "That's not funny. That's—"

"I know," she cut in, her voice frayed. "The more he ridiculed me, the more I worked. I worked myself to the bone trying to make a name for myself. I wanted to prove ..." Her voice felt broken as she finished the last part. "I guess I wanted to prove that it was worth it. That *I* was worth it. But it wasn't. It never was. So I closed it, or at least, tried to."

She curled her fingers into tight fists at her sides. "Until Davis realized how much he wanted to keep it, and refused to take it out of his name. Said it was his idea all along. And guess what? His new girlfriend is his lawyer."

A long silence stretched between them. Puffcake, sensing Eliza's sadness, fluttered over to her shoulder and curled up on it like a purring cat. She reached up and stroked his spine, her gaze absent.

Lachlan didn't speak, didn't try to give advice or half-hearted platitudes. He didn't offer up anything.

Instead, he just looked at her. Not as something broken, or to figure out, but as someone worth listening to.

"He's out of his mind," Lachlan said at last. "He's got no idea what he lost." He took a step forward. "And if I've learned anything about people who hurt others on purpose, it's that their actions say more about them than they do about you."

Eliza blinked, letting the words sink in. "I just can't imagine doing something like that to someone you're supposed to love." Tears now filled her eyes.

"*You* can't imagine doing that to someone you love because you would never do it to anyone. Even to someone you hate. You're nothing like him, Eliza. You're good. That's why it hurts."

Her throat tightened. Lachlan had used her first name when referring to her, not her last. It was like a match that lit from inside her chest, spreading throughout her entire body.

She looked down at her hands, getting an idea. "I'm going to name the scones '*Winter Hearth Scones.*' Because they remind me of that kind of warmth. The kind you don't expect, but once you feel it, you never want to lose it. What do you think?"

A grin grew across his face. "I love it."

She wasn't sure when she'd started enjoying his company, much less *opening up* to him. But now that he was here, listening, it all felt right and warm and oddly familiar, the same way Puffcake nestled into her shoulder felt right and warm and oddly familiar too.

"Lachlan?" She breathed his name, voice low. "Thanks for sticking around."

"There's nowhere else I'd rather be," he whispered.

Their eyes met and held. So many unspoken things hung between them that felt communicated in one single look. Gratitude. Recognition. Understanding. Longing.

Eliza blinked fast, trying to combat the tears. Lachlan noticed and smiled, trying, in his usual way, to lighten the mood.

"And if we're being honest, I've been sneaking seconds like there's no tomorrow. If you were mine, I'd be just fine with you 'playing housewife' any day of the week. May need to up my gym time, but I'll manage."

Those words made her heart beat stupidly in her chest. *"If you were mine."*

As if on cue, the oven dinged. The scones were finally ready for tasting.

Eliza slid on her oven mitts quickly, eager to focus her attention on something else. She opened the door, and a wave of cinnamon-spiced air wafted out and filled the cottage with its redolent warmth. The scones were golden brown and looked like a picture in a magazine. She snapped a photo of them before Lachlan or Puff-cake could grab one.

"Moment of truth," she anxiously said, watching Lachlan's every move as he took the first bite. He chewed slowly and closed his eyes as if he needed a second to process his thoughts.

"Snow ..." There was something reverent in his tone. "This is *perfection*. This is thirteen out of ten."

"Really?" Her voice jumped an octave, pride blooming in her chest. "You really think so?"

She reached for half of the broken scone and took a bite. The crisp, golden dough crunched slightly before the orange and cranberry notes burst in her mouth. It was the kind of taste that curled around your belly like a scarf.

It wasn't just perfect. It was delicious and magical and sweet. And it was entirely hers. For the first time in a long time, it was enough.

Chapter Fourteen

A Curse in the Crumbs

Outside, the snow pressed against the windowpane and muted the kitchen in a hush. Eliza leaned against the counter, covered in flour and satisfaction as Lachlan dried the last of the copper mixing bowls. It was the kind of quiet that Eliza loved when she was with company, and she wished it would stretch on forever.

"It's getting late," Lachlan broke the silence. "We should take a page out of Puffcake's book and get to bed. You're going to have a big day tomorrow."

Eliza followed his gaze over to Puffcake, who was sound asleep on a stack of recipe cards. She laughed, pulling out her phone and snapping a picture of him. "I'm definitely going to make a sticker out of this. Something with little floating Z's above his head."

Lachlan's laugh echoed through the kitchen, causing Puffcake to stir.

"Careful," she warned. "You wake the little sugar sprite, you'll have to deal with his wrath."

"What does that entail, exactly? Lighting my blanket on fire while I sleep?" Lachlan asked.

"Oh, worse," she said with a mock sort of seriousness, "He'll hex your coffee so it's always decaf."

Lachlan winced. "That's horrible. I take it all back. I'll start whispering from now on."

"You go ahead," she said, grinning as she pretended to shoo him off. "I promise I'll be right behind you, just want to do a couple more things before bed."

He lingered in the threshold, watching her for a beat too long. "Don't stay up too late," he said, voice gentle. "You'll need that little sugar sprite's magic tomorrow."

She pretended not to notice the warmth in his tone. "Go brush your teeth like a responsible adult," she teased.

He chuckled, shaking his head as he turned toward the hallway. His footsteps faded down the corridor.

Long after he was gone, she realized she was still smiling.

There was only one more recipe left. Eliza anxiously followed each of the instructions, her heart beating with a strange sort of anticipation. The recipe was for ginger-bread. *Simple enough*, she thought. And she was eager to use the rolling pin Lachlan bought for her from the little shoppe in the village square.

As she scanned the page, she noted the handwriting had shifted again. The once elegant script had grown uneven, less uniform, and more frantic. Blotches of ink stained the page in pools of onyx, like water or tears had spotted the words.

She worked in silence, careful not to disturb Puff-cake or Lachlan in the other room, but it was the recipe's twist that made Eliza stop stirring.

Add a tear.

She froze. She could've easily shed one for everything that had happened these past six months. But something about being here, spending the week away from it all, really gave her the distance she needed. It had given her perspective, and maybe even a newfound sense of hope.

Still, she couldn't stop the tears from forming as she thought about how she'd said goodbye to her nan too soon. She couldn't stop her hands from shaking anytime she thought about Honeycomb and who was at the front taking orders this holiday season.

It should've been her.

A single, pearlescent dollop welled onto Eliza's cheek. She caught it just in time as it slid down her face and into the dough. The moment it touched, the mixture shifted.

The recipe wasn't very clear on what, exactly, she was supposed to be recreating. She knew it was gingerbread, considering the classic nutmeg, cinnamon, and cardamom spices. But there were no specific notes on which biscuit cutters to use, or any shapes at all. Eliza took the liberty of cutting out ones shaped to look like a house, each one a small tribute to the magical cottage that kept her coming back year after year.

This place was full of memories, good and bad. Old and new. Watching Isadora's story unfold was bittersweet, and even though Eliza could assume how it ended, she wanted to keep baking to find out. She felt a strange bond with the woman, like she was reading about her favorite heroine and hoping that they would find happiness in the end.

Once the gingerbread biscuits were done and cooled, Eliza took a bite, and the cottage flickered around her like the hazy edges of a dream. She knew the feeling too well. She was no longer in her own story. She was in Isadora's.

And there she was: Isadora, hollow-eyed and wild-haired, kneading every ounce of anger into the pile of dough before her. With every knead, her fury seemed to soften into something more like despair. And from despair to hopelessness. Beside her on the counter was the letter from Ernest, unfolded and blotched with ink patches.

He'd left without a word. Only a letter left behind to account for all their years together, everything they'd suffered through. Everything was wrapped up with the words "*sincerely*" at the end.

The dough received the brunt of Isadora's grief, her knuckles turning white under her grip as she worked it with force. There wasn't a single trace of love in her baking now, only regret. Bitterness. Heartbreak rolled into spice and flour.

The scent flooded Eliza's lungs, cinnamon, sugar, clove, and molasses, but it was laced with the heaviness of sorrow.

"No one will know how much this cost me, but they'll feel it," she whispered, tears brimming in her eyes. Her voice was broken and ragged, like she'd been crying for some time, and this was her only consolation —this kitchen.

"Let this place remember," she said, speaking over the house as if she were cursing it. "Let this house carry the weight of what we had and the great loss. Sweet endings will never belong here."

She laid the gingerbread mixture out, rolling it out with swift movements. The pin moved back and forth like a metronome, a steady rhythm as she pressed all of her grief into the dough.

With trembling hands, she reached for the cutters. It was an odd set, not the typical ones shaped like stars or stockings. They were strange and curved. Eliza couldn't quite make out what Isadora was making until they were on the baking sheet.

As soon as she put the cutouts in the oven, the house shifted, the air becoming more stout with magic.

Then, shooting from the oven like a cannon, came a familiar creature. Golden brown and still steaming.

Eliza blinked. She didn't recognize him at first, but then she knew. There were undeniable pink and blue icing wings, batting experimentally, and two lavender gumdrop eyes.

A delicate snout huffed powdered sugar, and sparks flew, hitting the copper pots like a pinball, each of them gonging a loud *ding*.

Puffcake.

He was smaller, no larger than the size of a danish, and somehow more adolescent, as if magical gingerbread creatures could grow over time. But it was unmistakably him, Eliza's cantankerous, fire-breathing cracker companion. Brought to life eighty years ago, not out of joy or a magical whimsy, but out of heartbreak.

Had Puffcake found his way back here due to sensing Eliza's own heartbreak?

Isadora leaned over the counter. The sorrow in her eyes softened for a moment as she beheld the little creature. At last, he settled down in front of Isadora on the island. "There you are," she said in greeting, reaching forward to boop him on the nose. He hissed in his usual cranky tone, and Isadora laughed sadly.

"Even my own creations dislike my company." She blinked away her tears and tried again, stroking his spine. "Tell me you'll stay, won't you? You can't fix a broken heart, but surely you'll keep me company."

Puffcake curled into her hand in answer. Something in Eliza's heart silently broke, not only for Isadora, but for Puffcake, too.

Where was his lifelong companion now?

Then, she stood straighter, with authority. Her voice lowered, every syllable ringing out with the ancient weight of old magic. She spoke words that simultaneously created and changed everything.

"Let love not last here if mine cannot."

The spell rippled outward, sinking into every icing-piped rafter, every gingerbread wall, every sugar-spun flower and peppermint windowpane.

The house rumbled once, as if taking in its first—or final—breath.

Love hadn't just died within these walls; it had festered. What once had been a sanctuary for connection was now only a sad, withering memory; a graveyard for devotion.

And love, like the man who left her, would never return to this cottage.

"Eliza?" Someone was calling for her. It sounded far off in the distance, like she could run to it if only she could open her eyes from the spell she was under. She didn't want to go so soon. She wanted to sit with Isadora in her grief, even if she couldn't see or feel Eliza there.

"*Eliza*?" Her name came again. Closer now.

Someone was shaking her awake. The cottage around her swirled back into fractured pieces, first starting with sound, then light, and then, finally, feeling. Pine and sugar hovered nearby.

Lachlan was over the top of her, one hand braced underneath the base of her neck. The other was steadying her waist, his face drawn tight with worry. Beside him, Puffcake nudged at her arm, his caramel-colored scales glinting in the overhead light. The dragon's little lavender eyes were glossy with concern.

She blinked the rest of the way awake. The cool tiles were hard against her back, and there was a terrible throbbing in her head.

"Wh-what happened?" she croaked out.

"You fainted," Lachlan explained. "Puffcake woke me up."

She turned her head to the tiny familiar. "You did?"

Puffcake's gingerbread tail gave a proud *thump-thump-thump* in response.

Eliza reached out and scratched behind his ears, smiling brightly. "My little hero." Her comment only made Puffcake's chest puff wider.

Lachlan helped ease Eliza upright, steadying her. "Careful," he whispered, his voice gentle and almost tender. He drew his fingertips along her temple, checking for any damages. "No bleeding. That's good." He shone his mobile light in her eyes. "Follow my fingers, Snow."

She squinted, the brightness causing her head to pulse in angry protest. "I can't follow anything with how bright this light is in my eyes," she winced.

"Try for me," he whispered.

His hand tumbled slightly as they moved from side to side, testing her vision. She followed. Eliza tried to focus, but all she could think about was the closeness of him—the sharp evergreen clinging to his skin, the warmth of his breath. It wrapped around her like a spell.

He lowered the mobile. "Are you good?"

Eliza giggled. "I'm *fine*, Lachlan. A little dizzy, but fine. Just a little bump, that's all."

He studied her face, not seeming convinced. His eyes lingered on hers, gazing into them deeply. "You have the most brilliant eyes."

Eliza's breath caught in her chest. "Thank you."

He looked down at her lips. Her heart sputtered out of control in its usual manner around him. Puffcake nudged her cheek, breaking her away from the moment.

"I think he's trying to tell me it's time for bed," Eliza yawned.

Lachlan carefully scooped her up and carried her up the creaky staircase. His arms were strong, and she felt the muscle beneath his shirt as it strained against her weight. As he crossed the threshold and into the bedroom, the door behind them swung shut and shuddered closed with a soft click. Lachlan turned at the sound, his brows furrowing.

He gently set her down on the bed before crossing the room to inspect the door. He fumbled around with the handle, but it didn't budge. He just looked at it like it had personally insulted him.

He ran his hands through his hair. "I don't sleep around on the first date," Lachlan said, his tone half-embarrassed, half-flustered.

"I don't know if this would be considered a date," Eliza said.

"Isn't, like, this whole week considered that, whether we want it to be or not?" Lachlan pointed out.

"Touché," she smiled widely before nodding to the bed. "But really, we'd just be sleeping in the same room. Not ... well, you know."

"I know," he said quickly, sitting on the edge of the mattress. He made it a point to keep as much distance from her as possible, his shoulders tense. "I just was a bit much yesterday when we were decorating the tree," he confessed. His eyes found hers in the darkness, and they were softer now. "I respect you, Eliza."

Her throat tightened at the sincerity of his words. The warmth of his voice pulsed through the air like magic.

"Stay with me," she whispered.

He hesitated only a moment before joining her underneath the quilt. His breath was warm against the base of her neck, and she purred in delight as he ran his fingers lightly over her hair, continuously brushing the blonde strands away from her face. Her eyes fluttered shut.

She knew the choice wasn't really theirs to make, considering the house had already decided their fate. But the words were hers.

Entirely hers.

Chapter Fifteen

Christmas Eve Eve

A knock came at the door the next morning.

The sound sent Puffcake springing from his pillow, barking like a madman as powdered sugar fell from his wings. Eliza groaned sleepily, peeling herself away from the warmth of her slumber.

The other side of the bed was empty, and the door was wide open.

She smiled to herself as the memory of last night came flooding back to her in a tidal wave. She bit her bottom lip and followed behind Puffcake down the stairs to see what the matter was.

Gretel stood on the porch. She was bundled up in a

candy-pink jumpsuit that shimmered in the morning light. Her hair was in two French plaits that trailed down opposite sides of her head, with little sprigs of holly woven throughout.

Eliza tried opening the door, but, of course, the peppermint door handle wouldn't budge. It needed to be opened on its own terms. Eliza groaned again, although her heart sputtered at the thought of needing to find Lachlan to open it.

The fireplace crackled in response.

"Very funny," she called out to the house. She motioned to Gretel to give her one minute before padding down the hallway to search for Lachlan. He hadn't been in the kitchen and dining room, which meant ...

The bathroom door was closed, and steam billowed in wisps from beneath it.

"Okay, will you at least leave us a little dignity, please?" She asked the cottage nicely. But the cottage groaned something that Eliza was almost certain sounded like a "*No*."

Point taken.

She banged her knuckles on the door, "Um. Lachlan?"

"Yeah?" he called out over the noise of the running water.

"Gretel is here, and um, I can't ..." she hesitated. "The door is doing *the thing* again."

There was a beat. Then a chuckle as he shut the water off.

Seconds later, he emerged behind the door, and there he was, sopping wet with a towel slung low around his hips, his brunette hair clinging to his forehead. Steam curled around him like an inappropriate romance movie.

Definitely not in modest, Hallmark fashion.

Eliza's cheeks lit on fire. *Cursed house,* she thought. *It knew* exactly *what it was doing.*

Lachlan smiled, completely unbothered by his lack of wardrobe. If he noticed how uncomfortable she was, he didn't say so. "I didn't think you'd be up before nine, Snow. Even on contest day."

"Well, I *wouldn't* have been," she crossed her arms. "If it hadn't been for our visitor and Puffcake huffing, puffing, and threatening to blow the cottage down."

He barked a laugh, one of his rich ones that sounded like smooth butter. "Puffcake would make an excellent Big Bad Wolf, wouldn't he?"

"Tell me about it," she muttered, avoiding looking at his bare chest. "Now, could you please put on a shirt? Or at least dry off your body? You're going to make the house all soggy."

"Can't have that," he winked, closing the door.

By the time he emerged, this time in a t-shirt (thank Santa's shiny boots), Gretel had already found her way inside.

"Oh, come off it!" Eliza gawked at the house. "Do you thrive off of making us squirm?"

Gretel stood in the kitchen, making herself at home by helping herself to a biscuit from underneath the cloche. She whipped one of her thick plaits enthusiastically behind her back, an eyebrow raised. "Did I do something?"

"What? Oh, no, sorry. I was talking to the house, not you." Eliza explained. "It's been wreaking all sorts of havoc the past two days."

Gretel smiled mischievously. "Good."

"*Good*?" Eliza squawked. "Whose side are you on, Gretel?"

Eliza's friend gave her a look. "Don't tell me you're at least a *little* happy to be shacking up with him for the past week."

Eliza pursed her lips, looking guilty as she thought about it for a beat. "Okay, you got me there." She pointed at Gretel. "But that does *not* mean we're soulmates or going to ride off into the sunset together."

"And why not?" She just gave Eliza a look.

Eliza blinked. "Well, b-because we're—"

Gretel raised her brows. "You're …?" She popped out a hip. "I'll wait."

Eliza finally noticed the box sitting on the counter in front of Gretel. It was wrapped in festive baking-themed paper tied with pink lace.

She looked between the present and Gretel. "Is this for me?"

"No, for Lachlan." Gretel dramatically rolled her eyes. "Of course, for you! Who else would I wrap a gift in Candy Land-themed paper for? Merry Christmas Eve Eve!" Gretel greeted Eliza with a cheery grin, thrusting the gift in Eliza's arms. She leaned in close, lowering her voice. "But I know what you're doing, just so you know."

Puffcake narrowed his eyes at her as if to say, *Merry Christmas to you, too, Gretel.*

The sass in these dragon gingerbreads, thought Eliza. *Unreal.*

The warmth of the moment faded as she remembered the memory from last night. Puffcake had known companionship and love, too. And yet Isadora left him behind.

Eliza never remembered him from all her stays in the past. But that still didn't negate the fact that, for eighty years, he'd lived in the silence of this enchanted house, or alone somewhere on the property grounds. Had others who passed through offered him as much kindness and warm welcome as she had on the first day they met?

Even then, she hadn't been that welcoming of him. Not at first. She'd been more wrapped up in her own baking agenda. But now that she knew Puffcake, she couldn't imagine leaving him.

But was it only a matter of time before she left him, too?

She glanced down at the tiny gingerbread creation curled up around the base of her mug of hot coffee, his gumdrop eyes blinking up at her with sleepy indifference. She tried swallowing down the lump in her throat.

Temporary. Everything about this place was temporary. This holiday, the satisfaction of winning this baking contest, her newfound friendship with Gretel, her … *whatever* it was with Lachlan. Even Puffcake. What was she supposed to do after Christmas? Pack him up with her and head back to London with a gingerbread familiar? He might not even want to come. He might hate it there.

Gretel eagerly grinned, snapping Eliza out of contemplating. "Well? Are you going to open it, or am I going to have to sprinkle you with hurry-up pixie dust?"

Eliza snorted, pretending to be okay. "That is not a thing."

"Yeah?" She lifted a brow. "Have you looked through the magical spice rack?"

"And checked it twice," Eliza laughed, untying the lace. Her hands felt awkward as she peeled back the colorful paper, being stared at by everyone in the room. She always hated her own birthday parties. She felt like she was always meant to be lost in the crowd, not the one in the spotlight.

It was a baby-pink baking apron, and her name was delicately embroidered on the hem.

She instantly tied it around her waist, smiling from ear to ear. "Let's see if it gives me any luck in this contest. Thank you so much, Gretel. I love it."

"You don't need any luck when you're as good as

you are," Gretel complimented. "So don't let me down, kid." She clapped her hands once, rising from her chair. "Now, let's get that oven fired up. I'm ready to judge your scones."

"Are you really one of the judges?" Eliza asked, her heart leaping.

Gretel shook her head. "No, but only because I'd get accused of bias. Either way, I'm betting on your buns." She winked.

A slow grin spread across Eliza's face. She knew she liked this girl for a reason.

Chapter Sixteen

Kitchen Witches

As the scent of orange and cardamom filled the space, Eliza moved almost rhythmically through the kitchen, humming Christmas carols as she went. The new pink apron was already covered in flour and looked like it had been owned for years.

Gretel sat cross-legged on the breakfast table by the window, munching on a bowl of leftover sugared cranberries. She tossed them in the air, catching them with her mouth. She'd throw the occasional one at Puffcake, who would swoop through the air at an alarming speed to catch them just in time.

Eliza smiled to herself, comforted by their presence.

Lachlan was making himself busy chopping firewood in true Hallmark heartthrob fashion.

As Eliza baked, her thoughts turned pensive as she, once again, wondered about Isadora and the final memory last night. Her mind began to swirl like the cinnamon in her batter, slow and bittersweet. She got an idea.

"Gretel?"

"Hhmm?" answered through a mouth full of cranberries.

"You mentioned you've lived here since you were young, right?"

"Since I was knee-high to a biscuit jar," she wiped her stained hands on a napkin. She furrowed her lavender brows. "Why, what's up?"

"Do you happen to know if these cottages were built before ... say, the 1950s?"

"Oh, definitely before that. Like, way before that. These cottages are old. Storybook old."

"Tell me about it."

"Well, my dad always told me and Hansel that Gingerbread Hollow was once built by a coven of kitchen witches who were tired of getting burned at the stake just because they were good at cooking. Even though they used magic, it wasn't like they deserved to be killed." She shook her head and uncrossed her legs and began swinging both of them back and forth.

"So, they built their own adorable colony made of

sugar out in the middle of nowhere. Each cottage holds a different kind of magic. The kind that *remembers*."

Eliza thought of the incident Gretel told her about when she was a girl, and why she gets free rent for the rest of her life. "I don't mean to pry, but are you still staying in the cottage where the witch tried to ..."

"Oh, heavens no!" She laughed, and a wave of relief washed over Eliza. "That cottage is really haunted. For real. Lots of dumb college students stay there during October. They never last the evening." She shook her head. "We have our parents' old cottage. My mum is descended from the lineage of witches."

"Guess that explains the purple and blue hair," Eliza remarked.

Gretel giggled. "Guess so. Although I hope my hair fades stark white the way my mum's did. She'll be at the Reindeer Games tonight. She's typically in charge of the caroling."

"Have you ever heard any of the townspeople mention someone named Isadora?" she got bold enough to ask.

Gretel thought for a moment. "I ... can't say that I have."

Eliza just stared down at the dough she'd just rolled, her voice quiet but determined. "I think she lived here once. This house was once hers."

Gretel looked curious, waiting for her to continue. Meanwhile, Puffcake tried to nestle into the pouch of

Eliza's apron. She opened it for him, and he dropped inside.

"She was a baker, too, and she was in love. Except it didn't last. Her husband left her. Instead of screaming or throwing things, or doing the 1950s version of blasting him on TikTok, she just … *baked*."

Gretel squinted. "She got baked?"

"No," Eliza gave her a look. "She *baked*. With an oven, not edibles."

"How do you know all this?" Gretel asked.

"The house. Ever since I entered it, it's been showing me this cookbook. It isn't an ordinary cookbook—it was Isadora's. Once you bake the dessert and taste it, you see the memory she baked into it.

"She said, 'Let not love exist here if mine cannot.' And she meant it. The house changed after her. I think it's …" Eliza paused, thinking aloud. "I think it's longing to be redeemed. It's why the house only ever responds to couples. Or, in mine and Lachlan's case, two travelers. It wants the curse to be broken."

Eliza never considered this before now. Maybe the house wasn't trying to warn her, or even run them off from each other. Maybe it was offering her a chance to rewrite the narrative.

Gretel's eyebrows shot to her hairline. "Do you think you can do something about that?"

Eliza bit her lip, turning her head toward the window. She saw Lachlan place another log onto the cutting board and swing. The only sound in the cottage was the holiday music softly spilling from the record and Puffcake, who was already snoring away in her apron pocket.

"I don't know," she answered truthfully. Could love even blossom between the two of them this soon? She'd known him for four days. "I'm scared. I keep thinking … What if I end up like her? Like Isadora. What if I give everything, only for him to just leave?"

Gretel got up from her spot and joined Eliza at the island. "Then you'll know that it was real. You'll know you were brave enough to give someone the power to hurt you." She placed a hand on top of Eliza's and gave a small smile. "And if he tries to leave, we'll sic Puffcake on him."

Eliza let out a laugh and felt the tightening in her lungs loosen a fraction. Puffcake, on the other hand, was not amused because he was startled awake by the shaking of her shoulders.

The side door opened, and Eliza's stupid heart sputtered. Lachlan stomped off his boots and threw off his coat and hat, his hair messy and wild underneath. They locked eyes. For a moment, the house grew quieter, like it was waiting for something.

Eliza's timer on her phone buzzed. "Scones are done!" She announced, already reaching for the oven mitts. Perfect golden brown scones sat on the tray, the cardamom filling the cottage with the scent of Christmas.

Puffcake flapped his icing wings and made a tiny, excited screech.

Lachlan laughed, heading to the bathroom to freshen up. "They smell amazing. Keep up the good work, Snow. Maybe we'll bring home the gold."

Gretel's head snapped toward Eliza, her eyes wide. "*Snow*?" She mouthed, her hands flexed out in front of her victoriously. Eliza said nothing, but her blush grew a darker shade of crimson.

Eliza sprinkled coarse sugar over each of the scones. The sugar caught in the light of the steam, giving them a frosted appearance, like winter's first snow.

With delicate fingers, Gretel picked up each one and placed them inside the box. After tying a red bow around it, she looked up, giving Eliza a confident smile. "You ready?"

For a moment, Eliza hesitated. She wiped flour off her cheek with the back of her hand. "I think so. I just don't know if I can bear the rejection if I lose."

"That's the beauty about taking a chance, isn't it?" Gretel handed off the box like it was the holy grail. Then she winked, "It's much like falling in love."

Chapter Seventeen

Baking Spirits Bright

Lachlan came around the corner, dressed and ready. He wore a forest green shirt, a jumper, and matching socks with little Christmas tree cakes on them.

Their eyes met from across the room, and he gave her a warm smile. "I saved these socks specifically for this occasion." He stretched out on the couch, leaning back in the chair. "'Cause you're going to knock them right off later, Snow. I just know it."

Eliza blushed. She swiped open her camera to take a picture before quickly sending it to Piper, and the messages began rolling in.

Ding, ding, ding, ding.

ELIZA HE IS SO FIT 🔥🔥🔥

Looks like Hallmark Casanova's ready
to see you smash it!

Go on, girl! Show em who's best!

Eliza typed a quick thanks to Piper before locking
her phone.

"Hansel's on his way over," Gretel declared,
throwing her scarf back around her neck. "We'd better
get going. We don't want the scones to get too cold."

The snow crunched under four pairs of boots as the
group trekked their way to Gingerbread Hollow square.
The late-afternoon light cast a golden sheen on the
frosted thatch-roofed houses as Eliza nervously hugged
the box of scones, careful not to slip on a patch of ice.

The twins were up ahead, trying to push each other
playfully into the ditches filled with snow and fallen
leaves. Several paces behind, Lachlan walked next to
Eliza. Puffcake brought up the rear, snacking on the trail
of magical breadcrumbs.

The two of them walked in companionable silence
for a while, the wind nipping at their cheeks. Their arms
brushed every so often, sending threads of warmth up
her spine.

"So, I was thinking," Lachlan started, "After you win, we should celebrate. Nothing fancy. Just the two of us."

Puffcake blinked twice as if to say, "*Um. Hello?*"

"Okay, three of us." Lachlan rolled his eyes. Puffcake seemed slightly appeased, but not fully recovered from the comment. Now that Eliza knew about his history, she could understand why. She wasn't quite sure what happened to Isadora, but she'd known Isadora was long since gone by now.

Had anyone taken Puffcake in over the years, or was Eliza the first? She couldn't bear the thought. She couldn't imagine with his loving personality that she was the first, but it was an Airbnb place, after all. People came and went like a revolving door.

"*If* I win," she nudged Lachlan. "But what did you have in mind?"

Lachlan gave a half-shrug, "You'll have to wait and see *when* you win." He nudged her back to emphasize the last words. The confidence he had in her seemed to radiate off of him. "Surprises build character."

"Fine," she smiled. "Though I should tell you now, I hate anything that involves glitter, karaoke, or being the center of attention."

"Shoot," he frowned. "I'll have to cancel the skywriting telegram filled with parachuting exploding glitter bombs."

"Lachlan!" She shoved him harder.

"*Kidding.*" He grinned wider. "I do hate to break the

news to you, Snow, but you will be the center of attention when they call your name. Can you handle that?"

Her stomach did a little tumble. "I honestly haven't gotten that far. I imagine I'll do just about anything to win that grand prize." She sighed. "I just hope they're good enough."

"They're perfect," Lachlan reassured her, squeezing her arm. "Just like their baker."

Eliza hugged the box tighter to her chest. She didn't have to respond because up ahead was the glow of the Christmas Village. In the center of the square was a glittering three-tiered fountain, all the gingerbread buildings around decorated with string lights and glowing ornaments. A banner shimmered in the evening light, "*Welcome to the Reindeer Games!*"

Eliza's heart stammered when she spotted the tent with the sign "*Baking Spirits Bright*" above. She felt ready in a way she hadn't before.

Lachlan stopped her just before the opening. He looked at her, then, his brown eyes calm and reassuring. "I can't enter with you because you'll already have Gretel and Puffcake there with you as your helpers. But just know I'll be watching in the crowd. My eyes are on you, Snow. You got this." Then, he brought her in for a hug, careful not to tip the box in her hands.

Inside the tent was a vision of holiday splendor. Twinkling vintage lights hung above like colorful stars. The amalgamation of different baking dishes filled the air. Tables were decked out in crimson and green runners with grand poinsettia arrangements. Next to her, an old lady with hair the color of baking soda set up what looked like mini pecan pies.

"Mrs. Elle Toe's back at it again with the pecan pie. Bold move." Gretel whispered, her eyes scanning the room for Eliza's other competitors. "Who likes nuts in desserts?"

Eliza laughed despite herself. "Old people," she whispered back. Then she looked to the front of the room, where the judges were. All of them were old. "'Suppose she knows her target audience."

Her hands trembled as she unboxed her scones and carefully set them on display. Puffcake nestled himself in her new apron pocket. From across the aisle, Mrs. Elle Toe grinned widely, the lines cracking out in a fan along her eyes and lips. "What lovely-looking desserts," she complimented. "I don't believe I've seen you around before. I'm Mrs. Elle Toe." She stuck out her hand in greeting.

"Hi," she shook the elderly woman's hand. "Eliza Snow. My family and I come—*came*," she corrected, "here for holiday every year."

"Snow as in Marjorie Snow?"

Eliza's eyes lit up. "That's my nan. You knew her?"

"We go way back, dear." Mrs. Elle Toe patted Eliza on the top of her hand. "Will she be here later to watch the contest?" she asked.

Eliza's face fell. "Unfortunately not. She, um, passed away, actually. In July."

Mrs. Elle Toe looked genuinely sad. "I'm so sorry to hear that. Marjorie was a lovely woman. Never complained about anything." She leaned in close to Eliza, "Even when the baking was properly fudged. She used to be a judge in these contests ages ago."

Eliza bit her cheek, forcing the tears to stay hidden. A woman in a bright yellow suit jacket and matching trouser took the stage. Her long, ebony hair was braided into several thick plaits and twisted into a bun on top of her head.

She tapped on the mic to test if it was hot, and parted her cherry red lips into a smile. "Ladies and Gentlemen, welcome to the seventy-fifth annual Baking Spirits Bright competition! Bakers, please take to your tents and make your final touches. You have five minutes," she sing-songed the last part in a jolly jingle before tiptoeing off the stage.

"It was nice meeting you, Mrs. Elle Toe," Eliza smiled at the old lady. She wanted to stay and chat more with her about her nan. It felt good to hear old stories about her. "Oh, and good luck in the competition."

"Good luck, dearie! And Merry Christmas." She parted in a flurry, crossing the tent to her station.

Eliza did the same, and double-timed it as she began unboxing her desserts and setting it out on display. She set each of them neatly on the platter, careful not to fudge anything up. Once she was satisfied with her display, she took a step back, wiping her hands clean.

A man across the way from Eliza caught her attention. He appeared even older than Mrs. Elle Toe, which was saying something. He looked ancient. His hands shook as he slowly placed his Watergate Salad into a delicate glass bowl. His name tag read Frank.

Eliza checked the clock. They had only two minutes to go before the competition started. Frank was going so slow that she was sure he wouldn't finish his display in time. She stepped over and cleared her throat. "Excuse me. Would you like some help setting up? I don't mind."

Frank looked up, his glasses set low on his nose. He looked through them at her, his eyes looking twice as big through his particular lens prescription. "What'd you say?" he said, inclining his ear toward her.

She repeated herself, this time speaking much louder for him to hear. "Oh," was all he said.

Eliza had half the mind just to snatch the spoon out of his hand and begin shoveling it out for him. But Frank eventually slowly handed it to her, looking like a video using the slo-mo feature. Quickly, she scooped out the rest of the contents for him, and even put several cherries on top to further the appeal of the poor excuse of a Christmas dessert.

Who brings salad to a dessert competition? She shivered, feeling sorry for the judges who would have to test it.

Frank nodded his thanks before she rounded the table of her booth and took a seat next to Gretel. Puff-cake was sitting there, too, and gave her a disapproving glare. If he could speak, she could practically hear him saying, "*Frank is our competition, not a friend. Don't help him.*"

"It's the season of giving, Puffy. Lighten up." She scratched one finger under his chin.

Three judges made their rounds about the room, each taking their respective portions. After each bite, there was a thoughtful pause, followed by the *clink* of silverware, and several critiques filled with praise.

The woman in the yellow suit jacket was a judge, as well as another woman who was more petite with hair that looked too red to be natural. The third judge was a squat-looking man who hadn't looked like he smiled since the Thatcher years.

When they reached Eliza's table, she held her breath.

The youngest judge, the lady with the yellow suit jacket, approached first and politely introduced herself as Ruby. "Winter Hearth Scones," she read the card aloud. "Nice ring to it, yeah, Babs?" Ruby winked. "Let's see if they can withstand the heat of the competition here tonight, shall we?"

She plucked a scone before lifting it high into the air and clinking each of the other judges' scones like she was making a toast. Ruby took a bite. The other judges followed.

A hush fell over the entire tent. Eliza's hands felt numb. They trembled now as she looked down at them.

Then, Ruby snagged another bite, considering. "This is brilliant. A unique blend of zest and cranberries."

The second judge with flaming red hair just silently nodded. The third judge eyed the dessert under his spectacles.

Eliza made eye contact with Gretel and widened her eyes. *Oh God, they hate it.*

"I could've used a touch more coarse sugar or nuts to add that extra *crunch*," said the old man. For someone who tasted sweets all the time, he sure looked sour.

Eliza nodded, taking the critique with dignity. Beside her, Gretel fought not to burst out into laughter. Eliza bit her lip to keep from cracking a smile in the midst of this semi-serious setting.

When the judge turned away, Gretel leaned in, muttering, "He could use the extra sugar."

Finally, the judge with the red hair smacked her lips, and she placed her plate on the table. She dabbed her lips with a napkin. She looked at the nametag on Eliza's shirt. "Ms. Snow, is it? I never finish a dish. And I want seconds." She winked, wrote something down on her clipboard, then stalked away to the next contestant, along with the other judges.

Gretel nearly burst out into applause behind her. Eliza looked down at her scones, a handful still left on the table, and she began to feel her heartbeat slow.

The team of judges huddled together on the platform, murmuring amongst themselves. Ruby gave a curt nod before once again taking center stage.

Eliza caught Lachlan's eyes from across the room to find his were already fixed on her. He gave a smile, pulled out his phone, and typed.

Her phone buzzed. It was from Lachlan.

> Win or lose? You're the only one I'd want to be snowed in with.

Eliza blinked down at the message. Her cheeks bloomed with warmth despite the cold winter air coming through the tent's flaps. Her heart swelled with something that felt a lot like hope.

She just smiled up at Lachlan. *Maybe I wouldn't be so upset if I didn't win this thing, after all.*

Before she could type a reply, Ruby cleared her throat.

"A warm thank you to everyone for attending the seventy-fifth annual Baking Spirits Bright." Her tone was sharp but professional. "This year's entries were some of the most ambitious and delicious—" she turned toward Eliza and gave her a wink. "—we've had to date.

"Third place goes to Frank Mendel and his Water-Gate Salad." For a second, no one in the room said anything. Eliza looked to Frank, who was still looking up at the spokeswoman anxiously.

"Mr. Mendel," Gretel cleared her throat loudly. "It's you! You've won third place."

"Oh!" Frank scrambled to his feet. Gretel rushed

over to help grab his walker with tennis balls on the bottom.

"Second place goes to Mrs. Elle Toe and her Candied Pecan Pie."

Everyone in the room applauded. Mrs. Elle Toe waltzed up to the stage to receive her prize. When she came back, she cast Eliza a wink. "Good luck, honey."

Gretel grabbed Eliza's hand and squeezed; her lavender brows lifted high. "They've never in history both gotten outbaked. Eliza, I think you're—"

Eliza felt her stomach drop. The anticipation and the grand prize were all too much to bear. She held her breath, refusing to let disappointment claim her too early.

"And finally," Ruby continued, looking out over the crowd, "coming in first place …"

A pause.

"Eliza Snow and her Winter Hearth Scones!"

Gretel jumped up and down, squealing, and Puff-cake did a literal somersault in the air. Meanwhile, she just stayed quietly in place, stunned.

She'd done it. She won first place.

People cheered and clapped. She took center stage on the podium, her nerves fluttering like reindeer hooves on a rooftop. The trophy was handed off, polished, and shaped like a gingerbread man holding a spatula. Next, the woman in yellow handed her the over-sized check for her to snap a dozen photos with.

The weight of the trophy and the cardboard check

didn't feel real just yet. Suddenly, Lachlan was there, his hand wrapping around her waist. His voice was low and proud. "You won. Guess this means I owe you a celebratory surprise."

Eliza didn't have to fake her smile as she posed in front of the camera with Lachlan. Puffcake fluttered up onto Eliza's shoulder, his second-most favorite place to be aside from his usual mixing bowl sleeping arrangements.

A sudden ache came over Eliza as the realization crept in. It was two days before Christmas, and only three in total left before she and Lachlan packed their bags to return to their separate lives. She'd grown used to the sound of Puffcake's loud snoring next to her pillow every morning, the tiny weight of him as he settled on her shoulder, Lachlan's warm smile, and how it always seemed to find her.

What once felt like a temporary escape now felt dangerously like home.

Chapter Eighteen

Icing on the Cake

The entire group got a picture together before they made their way out into the open market, the village buzzing with laughter and caroling, with twinkling lights and decorated evergreens.

The village skating rink sat nestled in the center of the village, a huge fir tree lit up the space with a festive glow. Laughter echoed from families and couples already on the ice, wrapped in scarves and mittens.

Eliza tightened the laces on her borrowed skates and stood with a wobble. "Okay," she said, eyeing the slick surface with suspicion. "This is probably a bad idea."

"Too late," Lachlan said behind her, looping his

scarf around his neck. "You've committed now. No refunds."

"I've made a terrible mistake," she muttered as he took her hand and led her toward the rink.

He grinned. "Don't worry, I got you."

The moment her skates touched the ice, Eliza flailed like a newborn deer. "*Lies!*" she hissed, clinging to Lachlan's arm like a lifeline.

He laughed, steadying her. "You're doing great."

"There is nothing 'great' about this," she shot back.

They slowly began to skate—if it could be called that—with Lachlan gliding and Eliza mostly being dragged along.

"Why did I let you talk me into surprising me?" she demanded as they rounded the corner. "I should've known I was going to make a fool out of myself."

"An adorable fool," he grinned.

She looked up at him, her cheeks flushed from the cold and a little bit of embarrassment. "You're enjoying this way too much."

"I enjoy anything that involves you holding my hand," he responded coolly.

Eliza opened her mouth to say something in return but didn't get the chance. Her toe pick caught on a ridge of ice and she went flying forward. Lachlan caught her mid-fall, arms tightening around her waist as they both spun, landing in a heap near the edge of the rink.

They burst out laughing, faces inches apart. Their breath mingled in little clouds of winter air.

"You okay?" he asked, brushing a stray hair away from her face.

"Only emotionally hurt," she said. "And permanently humiliated."

"You're cute when you're humiliated," Lachlan said, his voice softer now. His hand lingered on her cheek, his thumb as light as a snowflake on her skin.

Eliza's smile faltered just slightly. "I think I like you too much," she whispered before she could stop herself.

His gaze flicked to her lips, then back to her eyes. "That's dangerous talk, Snow."

"Tell me about it," she said. She didn't move away.

For a moment, the world shrank. No snow, no rink, no curious onlookers. Just the hush of falling flakes and the soft beat of her heart in time with his. Then Puffcake came over and perched on the bench beside them. He let out a sharp, judgmental hiss.

"Saved by the sugar fairy," Lachlan muttered, helping her up.

Eliza smiled as they got back on their feet, her fingers still wrapped in his. And as they made another lap around the rink, she didn't mind the idea of falling.

Lachlan never let go of her hand as she managed to make her way around the rink a third time. Winded, they finally skated over to the edge to join Puffcake, who cheered them on from his designated spot on the bench.

"Best three laps of my life," Lachlan smiled, his cheeks flushed from the cold.

"And I only fell twice!" Eliza boasted.

Gretel skated over to join them, her lavender strands falling out of her braid. She offered Puffcake one of her roasted pecans.

Hansel joined them a few minutes later carrying two thermoses in his hands. He gracefully skidded to a stop and managed not to spill any of the steaming hot liquid inside. "For your journey home," he said, handing Lachlan and her each a cup.

Eliza took it between her hands, savoring the warmth. The steam rose to meet her cold skin, and she breathed in the crisp scent of apples. "Hmmm, cider," she breathed, "Thanks, Hansel."

Lachlan looked at his mobile, checking the time. "Which reminds me, we need to get going. Don't wanna be late to the next surprise," he winked.

The siblings said their goodbyes as Lachlan and Eliza exited the rink and headed toward the stalls to return their skates.

"*Two* surprises in one evening?" Eliza asked once they were alone.

Lachlan scooped up her gloved hand so casually, it felt as if he'd been wrapping his hand around hers for longer than just the evening. It was natural and smooth, like muscle memory. "I like you just a little bit, Snow."

His thumb traced a circle over a spot on her glove, a subtle gesture that sent warmth radiating through her.

"So, what is it?" She worked up enough courage to ask.

"You'll see. Just follow me."

Once they reached the town square, Lachlan took an immediate right, heading away from the music and busy streets. Puffcake and Eliza exchanged a glance.

"You do realize the celebration is the other way, right?" Eliza asked, arching a brow. She eyed the snowy, overgrown path ahead that led them back to their cottage.

He gave her a sideways glance and smiled. "Just a little romantic walk in the moonlight, Snow. Where's your sense of adventure?"

She laughed, falling into step beside him. She couldn't say she minded that they were headed back to the cottage. She was quite "peopled" out after the day she'd had. "If this is the part where you reveal you're actually a Christmas serial killer, then I'm haunting you for the rest of your life."

"That's fair, I s'pose." He squeezed her hand. "No murders, I promise." Lachlan dropped her hand, turned to face her, and swept an arm toward the next surprise behind him.

A single horse with chestnut hair and a silver mane snorted as its harness jingled with every movement. The sleigh attached to him sat expectant in the snow, the thick blanket lay draped over the seat wide enough for only two people.

"You're joking." Eliza gaped.

"No jokes, Snow. I take my one-horse open sleigh rides very seriously." Lachlan grinned as he held out a hand to help her up. "No laughing all the way for us."

She raised an eyebrow, but her cheeks lifted in a smile as she slid her hand into his. "*Ha-ha-ha*," she sang in a jingle.

He helped her up and climbed in beside her, pulling the blanket over their legs. The sleigh lurched forward gently, the bells on the horse's harness jingled in a soft rhythm as they glided down the trail lined with snow-covered trees.

The stars blinked above them, the air cold and crisp on their faces, but the blanket and Lachlan's warmth beside her kept the chill at bay. Puffcake, nestled in her lap underneath the blanket, let out a tiny snore and twitched one of his cinnamon wings.

Eliza leaned back, letting the snowflakes melt on her lashes. "You know, for someone who claims to dislike Christmas, you're alarmingly good at festive gestures."

"I don't dislike Christmas. Just couldn't really find it in me to spend it with my family." He looked over at her. "Besides, you've had a rough year, too. You deserve nice gestures."

Her breath caught a little. "You barely know me."

"I know enough," he said quietly. "And I know what

it looks like when someone's afraid to believe in good things."

She looked away, heart twisting in her chest. "It's easier to believe they won't last."

"What if they do?"

Their eyes met, the sleigh gliding slowly through the trees as the snow swirled around them. She felt the answer rising in her, somewhere between her ribs and the place she'd tried to keep walled off.

Eliza smiled, eyes misty. "Remind me to thank the house later."

Lachlan leaned in, brushing her hair from her cheek. "Remind me to kiss you before this trip ends."

Her breath hitched. "What if you don't need reminding?"

He said nothing. Just smiled.

The sleigh kept gliding through the forest back to their cottage, and for the first time in a long time, Eliza didn't feel like running.

Chapter Nineteen

The Great Flour War

Lachlan and Eliza stumbled inside the gingerbread house, breathless from laughter. The door locked shut behind them with a gentle thud as they shed their boots and scarfs by the door.

Puffcake carried the extra box of scones inside, clasping the red ribbon between his claws. Lachlan flipped on the light switch, and a soft amber glow spread throughout the room and danced over the icing-piped rafters.

The house seemed to sigh in relief now that the two of them were back inside. Even the fire in the hearth flickered more vibrantly, the Christmas tree glowed brighter.

"So … how about a nightcap?" Lachlan asked.

"Obviously," Eliza said, already moving to the kitchen. "Only if there's biscuits and peppermint bark, too."

Puffcake perked up at Eliza's suggestion. "I'll brew the chai, properly spiced. I know the perfect recipe," Lachlan smiled. "We make a good team, Snow."

Lachlan stepped behind Eliza to get into the fridge, his arm brushing up against hers. They moved around the kitchen together, their steps unhurried and rhythmic. His touch seemed to linger when she stepped in front of him, and he placed his hand on the small of her back to go around her.

Snow began to fall beyond the house, and Eliza smiled to herself, thankful for the magical storm that happened the day she arrived here. "Today was kind of perfect," she reflected, gently placing the bowl of melted white chocolate down on the counter.

"Yeah?" Lachlan got the bourbon from the liquor cabinet and tilted a dash into each of the steaming mugs.

"Yeah," she breathed. She turned to face him. "And you're to blame for, like, ninety percent of that, Lachlan. Thank you."

He placed his hands on each side of the counter and looked at her. Really looked at her. "I'm really proud of you, you know. For crushing the contest. After the year you've had, you could've just tucked your tail instead of putting yourself out there and risk facing rejection again. But you didn't. That was a really brave thing to do."

She snorted. "You talk about my life as if I'm a cancer survivor."

He set down his mug, ignoring her deflection.

"No," he said, "I talk like someone who knows what it's like to be gutted by the person who was supposed to love you and still finds the courage to try again."

Eliza opened her mouth, but couldn't seem to find the right words.

"You didn't have to come here. You didn't have to bake, or sign up for that contest, or let yourself feel anything again. But you did. You got back up and put your heart into something again. That takes guts, Snow."

She glanced away, unsure how to hold his gaze. "To be fair, Gretel entered me into the contest. I just made the pastries, I'm not exactly a war hero."

"You're *my* hero," he placed his hand to his chest. "You slayed at least three metaphorical dragons this week and tamed an actual one with gingerbread wings."

She laughed despite her tightening throat. "I wouldn't say I *tamed* him."

Lachlan stepped closer to the island, leaning casually against it. "Still. Takes guts to win over a sentient sugar biscuit."

"Oh, hush," Eliza giggled, booping Lachlan on the

nose with her flour-coated finger. "You know Puffcake chose *me*."

Lachlan blinked. "Did you just boop me on the nose?"

Another flurry of giggles escaped her. "You look like Rudolph. Rudolph the powdered nose."

"Careful, Snow," he said, inching closer to the mixing bowl. "That sounds a lot like a challenge."

"What are you doing?" she asked as she watched him grab a handful of the flour. Seeing the mischief in his eyes, she cocked her head. "You wouldn't *dare*."

"Oh, I would." He grinned.

"You even think about throwing that and you'll wake up tomorrow morning with marshmallow cream in your shoes."

"I accept those terms."

Before she could dive for cover, a puff of flour launched across the counter, hitting her square in the chest and face. She gasped, coughing and blinking through the cloud of powder. Her apron, sweater, and hair were completely covered in white.

"Oops," Lachlan shrugged innocently.

Eliza wiped a slow hand down her front, then fixed him with a deadly calm expression. "You're a goner."

He grabbed some more flour from the bowl before backing away from her. "*What*? You said marshmallow cream! I was prepared for a mild inconvenience, not mortal consequences!"

She launched herself forward, reaching into the

mixing bowl and grabbing a handful. She struck him straight in his smug face. It hit with a satisfying *pouf*, coating his jaw and the front of his dark henley.

He coughed. "Snow! I am *drenched*!"

She gave a smug expression. "Now we're even."

"Oh, no we're not. You just started a flour war." He threw another handful at her, this time pelting through the air and raining onto the counters like snow.

And in a flurry of shouts, they ducked behind the island and flung handfuls across the room like they were snowballs.

Puffcake let out screeches of joy as he looped between them, pretending to act as a referee with a spatula between his claws. The bowl sat in the center of the island like a powder keg.

Getting an idea, Eliza popped from behind the counter and reached for the entire mixing bowl to take it away from the middle. Lachlan lurched forward to stop her, his hands on either side of hers. "Foul!" he protested, "Puffcake, call it!"

In his excitement, Puffcake blew out a tiny gale of fire, scorching one of the cabinets. Eliza slipped, and the next thing she knew, she was falling backward, the mixing bowl coming with her. The back of her head hit the cabinet with a thud, and the rest of the flour mix spilled into her lap.

She reached for her head, half-laughing and half-wincing from the pain. Before she knew it, Lachlan was there beside her. "Are you okay?" His voice turned gentle. His hand reached for the top of her head, cupping it in his hands.

"I'm okay," Eliza reassured him, breathless from the fight.

Both of them were covered in white, their hair and clothes dusted in flour. Puffcake settled himself on the counter and began doing snow angels in the aftermath.

She looked up and met his eyes. They were warm and full of concern. She realized how close they were together now on the flour-coated floor. She took in the scent of evergreen, coffee, and cinnamon.

"I'm sorry. I think it's my fault," he apologized.

"It's no one's fault," she breathed. "I slipped."

He tightened his lips into a flat line, as if relishing telling her the truth. "Well, I may have let go of the bowl …" He quickly continued, "but I didn't think you'd fall back and hit your head. It was a stupid move. I shouldn't have done it."

Eliza only smiled. "It's something I would've done, too." She looked at the wreckage of the kitchen, the layer of white dust that coated everything. Puffcake had left little snow angels on the counter.

Even her golden trophy wasn't spared from the debris. It sat over by the baker's rack covered in white.

Suddenly, tears welled in her eyes.

"What is it, Snow?" Lachlan's hand caressed the back of her head as he surveyed her eyes.

"It's nothing. It's just that I haven't—" she sniffled, feeling pathetic for even finishing the thought.

"Haven't …?" Lachlan pressed.

She rolled her eyes briefly, looking away from him. At last, she worked up the courage to speak her mind. "It's just that I haven't had this much fun in a really long time."

But it was more than that. She loved Lachlan and Puffcake's presence. She wasn't ready to venture back into the mundane reality of her bleak and boring life. Sure, she now had the money to at least help start her new bakery, but it still wouldn't feel right.

It wouldn't feel right without them.

And it felt like each day the hour hand on the clock ticked by faster. Her remaining time was wearing thin.

"I don't want to leave this place," she whispered. *I don't want to leave* you, she wanted to add.

"I don't either," Lachlan admitted at last. His hand drifted around to cup her cheek, his thumb brushing her jawline. The movement felt so natural that Eliza wasn't even nervous now that he was this close. She just felt … *Ready*. Eager. Willing.

Lachlan's brown eyes swept down to her lips. He gently brushed a hair away from her face. Puffcake covered his eyes from inside his designated mixing bowl as Lachlan leaned forward.

Eliza's heart raced wildly in her chest, anticipation and yearning seeming to freeze every cell in her body. Ever-so-slightly, his lips pressed into hers. Their kiss felt like the joy of Christmas morning, the start of something magical and new. Like running down the stairs to find heaps of gifts and the smell of fresh biscuits.

Lachlan moved his hand to the back of her neck, their breathing mixing and mingling. He kissed her thoroughly, exploring every facet, taking his time. She didn't think about the future, but only the here and now. She wouldn't rush this moment. Wouldn't let it slip by. She needed it to last forever, even though she knew all things came to an end.

This time, she hoped—believed, even—that it might last.

The house even seemed to glow a brighter shade of amber, and the colorful lights on the trees twinkled a more vibrant hue. At last, they looked up to see the same emerald green piping with icing berries the color of crimson.

They both laughed, resting their heads together.

Then, there was an abrupt knock on the door that startled them both. Eliza rose to answer it, but Lachlan motioned for her to stay put. He swung the door open, and Eliza saw the dark blond cropped hair even in the dim porch light. His green eyes looked between Lachlan and hers, fury written on his face.

"Davis?"

Chapter Twenty

Broken Hearts and Sugar Glass

Davis didn't bother with pleasantries. He never had, because he was apparently above them. He perused Lachlan up and down, and back up again, his lip curling in disgust. "Really, Liz? This was the best you could do for a rebound?"

Lachlan didn't flinch. If he was hurt, he did an amazing job at covering it. He gave Davis a friendly grin, but there was a cold recognition in his eyes.

"I'm sorry, mate," Lachlan responded coolly, stepping slightly in front of her. "But I think you should leave." His posture wasn't threatening, only protective.

Davis's eyes darkened. "I don't answer to you."

"Maybe not," Lachlan shrugged, "But you've done enough. She came here to get away from everything, not for it to follow her."

Davis's gaze cut to Eliza, sharp as broken glass. "So that's it?" You ran away to your nan's fairytale cottage to play house with the first guy who smiled at you since I broke up with you? To forget about real life and big girl responsibilities?" His voice dripped in mockery, his jaw set. "Too busy with him to answer your mobile?"

A lump formed at the base of her throat, and she was unable to reach his eyes. "Signal's been spotty," she murmured. Her voice wavered as she spoke, but she still said, "You need to leave, Davis. Now."

Davis ignored her completely. His focus tunneled in on her, and his tone shifted as if on cue, like he didn't just tell her off for having company at her supposed-solo spot. "Liz, can we just talk in private?"

Lachlan glanced over toward Eliza. He looked worried for her, yet acquiescent to her decision nonetheless. She swallowed hard. The idea of being alone with Davis made something in her stomach twist. "I think whatever you have to say, you can say in front of us both."

Davis narrowed his eyes, jaw flexing again. "You're joking, right? You leave for holiday for a week, and suddenly this guy is making decisions for you?" He laughed bitterly. "Unbelievable."

"Look," Lachlan interjected, running his hands through his hair. "I'm not making decisions for her. She clearly was the one who said she didn't want to be alone with you. So just respect it, mate."

Davis shot him a glower. Then he blinked slowly, turning his attention back to Eliza. "Well, I came this way to tell you some news. I guess I'll have to deliver it in front of both of you since you don't want to be alone with me."

Her stomach took another nosedive in anticipation. She couldn't handle any more bad news this year.

"Look, Liz," Davis began. He blew out a breath and knitted his brows together. He almost looked worried to tell her the news. "I came to tell you that Katie lost the business. We didn't know what else to do. We had to close it. I know how much Honeycomb meant to you. I just tried to keep it going for your sake." Deliberate or not, Davis's voice cracked. "And since Katie and I broke things off, it's made me realize how much I really missed you."

"Don't." She cut him off, blinking rapidly through the tears. Her throat ached as she tried to make sense of his words.

Honeycomb was just *gone*? The bakery had been her dream. Her passion. Her *life*. All those late nights, all those months of preparation and hiring. Setting up a social media account and pouring every last shred of her identity she had left into it. And it was gone.

Her hands trembled. The burning in her chest hurt worse than just grief—no, it was *fury*. Fury that Davis had waited until now to tell her, once the doors were closed and it was all said and done with. Fury that he thought this performance would earn him any bit of sympathy from her. Fury that Davis had just admitted to her being an actual rebound.

Before she could stop herself, the words came rising out of her chest. "Do you honestly think that counts as an apology? I mean, do you really expect me to take you back after everything you put me through? You took the bakery from me and then *lost it*. And then you show up here unannounced, and find a problem with the fact that I'm staying with someone else? I'm sorry, but you've lost the right to hold me accountable for my decisions six months ago when you decided to step out on *me* for another woman. You don't get to rewrite any of the rules after you break them." She shook her head, her entire body humming with anger. "But that's just it. The rules were never for you, were they?"

"Oh wow, there it is." His expression went cold and unrecognizable. "You just love playing the victim when it's convenient. Like you didn't make choices too. You were always away and busy. If it weren't for that, you might not have pushed me away."

"I was helping take care of my dying grandmother!" Eliza yelled. She felt her rage climbing higher and higher. She just wished he would *leave*.

He scoffed, like her grief was an excuse he was tired of hearing. "I'm not saying she wasn't sick, but I'm saying you left me. You always made me feel like I was last on your list. So what was I supposed to do, wait around while you had your life everywhere else but with me?"

Davis took a step forward, snow crunching on the doormat. "So don't stand there acting all righteous. I came here to fix this, and you're the one having random men over just to hurt me."

Lachlan's arm instinctively reached out, blocking Davis's path from stepping any further inside. Puffcake arched his back and hissed steam out from his nostrils.

"Easy, Puffcake," Lachlan said.

Davis looked down at Lachlan's hand. He ground his teeth as he slowly said, "Get your hand off me."

All around them, the cottage gave a deep, low rumble.

"Careful," Eliza warned. "The house might retaliate."

Davis scoffed. "The *house*? Are you hearing yourself?" He let out a humorless laugh. "You have officially lost it, Liz. Maybe you and your new boytoy can bake up a nice batch of delusion together, if you haven't already."

He whirled around toward the baker's rack, and snatched up a snow globe. Inside, little gingerbread men danced around a tree, glitter raining down from the sky. Davis held it up in his hand. "You think this place has magic or something? Let's test that theory."

Before anyone could stop him, he hurled the snowglobe at the sugar-spun window. Shards of sugar and ice shattered in a thousand fragments. The temperature dropped instantly. Outside, the wind howled.

Then, the floorboards began to quake beneath them. A gust of magical wind tore through the open doorway, yanking Davis backward so violently that his heels skidded—then he slipped clean out of his shoes. The abandoned footwear hit the floor with two dull thuds as he was pinwheeled through the air into the vortex of snow. His eyes were wide with terror.

A heartbeat later, the shoes shot after him, launched by some unseen force. They tumbled end over end in the snow after him. Lachlan braced a hand against the harsh weather, "Hey, mate! Don't forget your shoes."

But Davis couldn't hear anything over the wind and his own voice as he shouted, "This isn't over, Liz!" It was high and shrill, sounding too much like a screeching wicked witch in her failed attempt at revenge.

Eliza stood at the threshold. Her hair and the tassels on the end of her scarf whipped wildly all around. She lifted a shaky hand, trying to bat the stray pieces away. Her pulse thundered in her ears, her adrenaline causing what seemed like every part of her body to tremble. This time, she was no longer scared of him, just free. Truly free—and quite amused.

"Oh, I think it's been over for a long time now!" she yelled back.

The door slammed shut for her, and the lock clicked into place, but not before Puffcake blew a huge, defiant raspberry at Davis as he floundered in the snow. The silence that followed was almost palpable.

Eliza's knees buckled from beneath her. She buried her head in her hands. Tears came quicker than she would've liked to admit.

"Hey, hey, hey." Lachlan rushed over, his voice featherlight. "You're okay. He's gone."

"That was so humiliating," she sobbed. "I can't believe I dated that foul toad. I didn't even know he could find me here. He must've saved the address's location from before. He just—showed up."

"You don't have to apologize." Lachlan brushed a tear away from her cheek with his thumb. "You didn't do anything wrong." His upper lip hitched a crooked smile. "Besides, I think he's the one who got humiliated. Poor bloke'll have a hard time trudging back home in all this snow if he doesn't find his shoes."

Eliza couldn't help but smile at the humor of it all. At last, she blew out a breath. "I just hate you had to get all wrapped up in this."

"*Wrapped up*?" Lachlan repeated gently. He bumped her shoulder, trying to coax a smile. "What's Christmas without a little chaos?"

That earned a small laugh.

Puffcake flew over to Eliza's side, nudging her with his snout, then curled into her lap. His little body was as warm as a loaf of fresh bread from the oven.

"I'm proud of you," Lachlan whispered. "For the

contest, for facing that little shoeless tosspot and standing your ground."

She met his eyes. There wasn't any judgment there, only awe. He truly meant it. "Thank you."

She craned her neck and planted a kiss on his cheek. He turned toward her, cupping her face and capturing her lips in a slow, gentle kiss that took her breath away. He tasted of the lingering sweetness from the scones and hot chocolate they'd shared earlier that evening.

For the first time in years, Eliza didn't feel small. She didn't feel like someone's mistake or second best. She felt … possible. She felt the weight of that possibility, a future she hadn't dared to imagine, but only hoped she could find one day.

Outside, the snow drifted in soft, swirling spirals, catching in the kitchen light like falling stars. She thought to wish upon one of them, but something like anxiety swelled in her chest. Davis's presence had caused the doubt to sprinkle its way back inside.

Beginnings always came to endings, did they not? As their remaining hours dwindled and their stay slipped closer to its ending, a single question plagued her. What would happen when the week was over?

Chapter Twenty-One

Ashes in the Gingerbread Hearth

Eliza yawned as she slipped out of bed. Today, she was the last one to rise, with Puffcake and Lachlan already up and in the kitchen.

Puffcake's wings were batting away as he used his claws to dump batter over onto the cooker. The thick cream slowly oozed onto the pan with a soft sizzle. Lachlan nodded his thanks, spatula in hand and shamelessly wearing Eliza's apron again.

"Careful there, Puff," she said as she moved toward the coffee pot. "You're going to burn yourself medium rare."

Lachlan snickered; however, Puffcake didn't like the

idea of being the object of someone else's joke. He let out a little puff of smoke in answer.

"That's fair, you are somehow a fire-breathing, sugar-huffing edible dragon," she replied.

"Merry Christmas Eve," Lachlan moved around the island to Eliza, pulling her close to him. He smelled like his usual evergreen scent mixed with batter.

"Lachlan, I thought we had an understanding to leave the baking up to me." She looked up to find him already smiling down at her.

"I know, but that doesn't mean I don't want to do sweet things for you from time to time."

He leaned in, pressing a gentle kiss to her forehead before planting a second kiss on her lips. He kissed her the way one savored the first bite of dessert—slow and reverent, and sweet on the tongue. Taking it all in, as if the moment itself was perfectly warm and golden; too precious to rush, and too perfect to waste.

Lachlan broke away abruptly, resuming his duties over the cooker. "Gotta get back to breakfast. Don't wanna be two for two in burning anything," he apologized quickly.

He flipped the pancake, and Eliza finally got a good look around the house.

The broken window had magically fixed itself overnight, and the snow globe was back inside, sitting on the shelf. It was like all traces of Davis were gone— except for the lump of uncertainty in her heart.

The house seemed to glow a bright shade of amber,

the multicolor string lights of the evergreen mixing their vibrant hues around the house like a kaleidoscope of color. Along the hearth were three knitted stockings. And on the counter was *Isadora's Memory-Baking Cookbook*.

"W—where did you get that?" Eliza asked nervously.

Lachlan didn't look up from his work, only smiling to himself. "They were hung up when I woke up, too. Thought you must've created that touch, but I guess I was wrong."

"Not the stockings," she swallowed. Her finger shook as she pointed to the cookbook. "*That*."

He followed her gaze. "Oh, just from the cupboard where the rest of the cookbooks are. You haven't used this one yet? Figured you'd have blown through all of the recipes in every cookbook here so far—"

"That's the thing … I have." Eliza said, "There's no recipe for American pancakes in Isadora's cookbook." She'd baked the last recipe in the cookbook two evenings ago.

What was going on? Did the cookbook reveal another recipe? When they eat the pancakes, would they both see another memory? Would it somehow unlock another sad flashback of Isadora's life?

"Yeah, there is," Lachlan protested, shrugging it off. He didn't seem to catch her uneasiness. After all, why would he? He hadn't been the one to see the memories within the recipes. "Page 13. It flipped straight to it for me. It's like the house *wanted* me to bake this for you. Any particular reason?"

"They're my favorite."

Lachlan just stared at her before bursting into laughter. "Of all the astounding, literal award-winning desserts, American pancakes are your favorite. You surprise me every day, Snow."

"It was the first thing my nan taught me to make," she said softly.

"Is that so?"

She nodded, the memory of her nan ebbing away the moment of anxiety due to the cookbook's presence. "Right here, in this gingerbread house."

"Well, I know I'm nothing like the Snows, but I hope my efforts are acknowledged."

She smiled. "I'm sure they'll be fine. Besides, it's the thought that counts."

Puffcake fluttered over to her, beckoning her to take her seat at the round table. She sat, sipping her coffee, and Puffcake continued to help Lachlan bring the bottle of syrup and napkins over to the table.

She wondered what memory they were about to experience. Her fingers itched to get a hold of the recipe, to see what the title of the dish was, if she could at least have an idea as to what she was about to witness.

"What's the name of the pancake recipe?" she asked. "Each recipe in this cookbook has an *interesting* name."

Lachlan glanced at the book. "Holly Jolly Hotcakes. Festive, huh?"

"Festive," she repeated. It didn't sound like one of the more solemn recipes, like *Silent Night Soufflé* or *Barren Cradle Bake*.

Lachlan lit the taper candles in front of her before placing her plate in front of her. They were perfectly round and fluffy, still steaming from the hot frying pan.

Seems Lachlan *was* good at cooking one thing. She smiled to herself, thankful that it was *pancakes*, of all things. She could certainly get used to this. She drizzled the hot syrup on top and sliced off a piece, eager to try it. Then she stopped herself, remembering the magic attached to the dessert.

Bracing herself, she popped it into her mouth.

She closed her eyes, breathing in the gingerbread house. Her hesitation then gave away to savoring, and then to bliss. She closed her eyes, and there, she saw her. Her nan, standing in the gingerbread house in her apron, her hair an icing white. The whisk was stirring itself as she poured buttermilk into a measuring cup, her crystal blue eyes aglow the way they always were when she was baking something.

Her nan dropped a bit of icing on her shirt, just shy of where the apron didn't cover, and she giggled to herself.

Eliza opened her eyes. They were wet with tears. She remembered that laugh. It was good to hear it again.

It wasn't a memory of Isadora's, but of her own. It

hadn't been the magic that made her remember. No, it was the nostalgia of the flavors. They'd just ... taken her back.

She wished she could've stayed there with her a little longer.

Instead, she took a second bite of her pancake. Then a third and fourth, until the entire thing was gone. The memories came flooding back to her, not quite as strong as the first one, but they were there all the same.

Lachlan's laugh broke the silence. He nodded to the empty plate. "I take it that I met your standards?"

Eliza smiled back. "In more ways than one. Thank you for that."

She rose to take her plate to the sink, but Lachlan stopped her, coming over to take it for her. "No, please. Let me." He placed a kiss on her cheek before returning back to his seat. "This is for all the times this past week you've served me."

"Wasn't that the deal?" she asked. "I serve you sweets if you keep quiet?"

"It was. Turns out you liked my presence more than you let on."

"Just a little bit."

She was curious, now, about the cookbook. So she reached over for it and scanned the particular ingredients. It was weird. This recipe was completely normal, void of any exact phrasing, measurements, or extremely particular directions that would warrant it to be a magical recipe. It was just plain old American pancakes.

So why had the memory felt so strong, so alive? Was that just the magic of the memory, how strongly connected she felt to this dessert that it brought her back to another time, another place, entirely her own?

And what about Lachlan? Why had this cookbook revealed itself to him when it did? Why *this* recipe? It was like the house knew that pancakes were her favorite, and it'd saved them specifically for this moment.

"You're quiet," Lachlan sipped from his cocoa with ease.

"Yeah," she admitted, looking out the window. The sun was pouring in through the sugar-spun glass, casting an array of colors throughout the kitchen.

Why was she so in her head about all this? It was Christmas Eve. It was supposed to be a happy day. One she planned to spend with Lachlan and Puffcake, binge-watching happy Christmas movies.

But in two days, they'd be gone from here. She couldn't shake that part of the deal, either. And with Isadora's cookbook laying out, paired with the random arrival of her ex, it further drove the statement home that happy endings were rare.

There was a lot for her to think about today. A lot of questions that needed answering. There was no resolution with Isadora or her story. Did she ever find love again? Were they somehow able to start a family together, or had her new significant other loved her regardless of her ability to give him children? Or was that the point of all this happening, that it was to show Eliza that, despite her efforts, any love kindled here always was extinguished?

"Just thinking, I suppose," she added..

Lachlan raised a brow, suspicious. "You know, you don't normally think this hard when there's sugar and coffee involved. What's going on, Snow?"

She hesitated before setting her mug down. She needed to tell him. She'd been keeping the secret of Isadora from him for too long. "I've been baking all week … " she started.

Lachlan snorted. "Gained a few pounds to prove it. Tell me something I don't know."

"Well, I've sort of been … waiting to bake some things when you and Puffcake go to sleep," she confessed.

Lachlan cut his eyes at her, feigning a look of offense. "You mean you save some things for yourself?" He shook his head. "Even for you, that's cold, Snow."

She stopped him. "They were from this recipe book. It revealed itself to me the first night we came here. Just literally fell onto the floor behind me. It was like it was wanting me to pick it up from the shelf, and so that's what I did. I baked them while you and Puffcake were asleep.

"There were certain *memories* attached to each of the desserts. They were about a woman named Isadora." She tapped on the title page. "The first one came with a happy memory, about her and her husband. But after that, they became progressively sadder and sadder, until the last memory was the saddest of all. She was left by her husband because they couldn't have children together." A tear slipped from Eliza's eye. "Isadora's the reason this cottage is cursed. She cursed it when he left. She even made Puffcake because of it, too. She's the reason we can't leave here unless we're together."

He grabbed Eliza's hand from across the table. "I should personally thank her for her sorcery, then. It's because of her that we were brought together."

She bit her cheek, looking down at their conjoined hands. The soft ticking of the grandfather clock was the only sound between them. It reminded Eliza of one of the last memories in the cookbook, where Isadora was sitting all alone—in this very spot—with her palms buried in her face as she wept, the letter from her husband before her.

The feeling was so overwhelming, she had to look away. She felt sick to her stomach as she pulled her hand back.

His brows furrowed. "Eliza? Are you alright?"

"I guess I'm just trying to figure out what happens next," she said carefully. "After tomorrow, when all the magic fades."

"What do you mean?" He blinked.

She blew out a frustrated breath. "I *mean*, we've been living in a little enchanted bubble these past few days. Baking, skating, sleigh rides, flour fights ... whatever *this* is," she gestured between the two of them.

"But what happens when all this is over? What happens when we leave here and we drive our separate ways, leave these gingerbread walls behind?"

"We'll visit each other," he reassured her. There was so much confidence in his tone that Eliza almost believed him. He made it seem so easy.

"You live in another region, Lachlan," she reminded him. "I'm in London. You're in Littlehampton. You've got a career. I'm going to be building mine from scratch again, probably working insane hours just to make ends meet."

Lachlan shrugged, like he already had it figured out. "Five and a half hours is nothing. I could even pick up homes in the London area, and I'll help you out—"

"Yeah, and rely on you for funds? No thanks. I'm not asking for your help. Can you just cut the good guy act for two seconds?"

Lachlan looked taken aback. "You think I'm *acting*?"

Eliza met his eyes. "That isn't what I meant—"

"No, I think that's exactly what you meant." He rose from the chair, running a hand through his hair.

"I just meant that—I just think you might decide you find a better offer somewhere else, and then you'll be done with me. I'll go back to trying to rebuild what I lost, and pretending that I'm okay."

Lachlan went entirely still. Only his jaw popped in and out a few times before he spoke again. "You seriously think I would do that?"

She opened her mouth to speak, but closed it again. After everything she'd recently been through, she'd just opened her heart again. She wouldn't be able to stand it if Lachlan decided to walk away, too. She shrugged. "I barely know you."

She saw the way the words landed, and she instantly regretted saying them. She wished for a rewind button, one where she could take it all back. What was she trying to do, exactly? Was she doing the classic "*push him away to see if he'll only lean in closer*" tactic? Because if so, she felt kind of pathetic in doing so. That doesn't happen in real life.

But there he was, still there. Still leaning on the kitchen counter across from her, trying to listen. Looking incredibly wounded, but still listening.

Her phone buzzed on the island, and she picked it up to check it.

Laurie

Would you want aisle seating or window? Merry early Christmas ;)

Booked you a train back early tomorrow. You deserve to end your awkward gingerbread house sabbatical on a high note.

Eliza simply stared at the messages. She didn't know a Laurie. And her phone case wasn't black—it was pink. And it wasn't her phone. It was Lachlan's.

"When were you going to tell me you were leaving?" Her hands shook as she twisted the phone around for him to see. She could barely get the words out. Betrayal laced around her heart like cold winter air. It felt like it had sunk into her lungs and weighed her down.

"What?" He knitted his brows together.

She tapped on the message, lighting up the screen once more. "Your sister. She texted you. Booked you a train, apparently. For tomorrow morning. So you don't have to stay."

Lachlan reached for the phone, reading the texts off for himself. He looked genuinely caught off guard. "She mentioned that the day after I got here, but I didn't think it was still a thing."

Eliza searched his eyes for any clues that he may be lying, not ready to give in so easily. "But you didn't tell her to cancel it earlier."

"I–I didn't think I needed to." He held his hands up in defense. "She mentioned it the first day I came here, but I reassured her it would work itself out and we'd get settled in different cottages."

"But when we didn't, you decided to ask her to book the first train ride you could out of here?" she asked.

He ran his hands through his hair, taking in a deep breath, before shrugging. "No. It wasn't a part of my agenda for my sister to book me anything."

Eliza thought of Davis and all of his schemes. His initial love bombing. She felt like she was being blindsided with the truth all over again. For two years, everyone had seen his red flags but her, apparently. She hadn't noticed any with Lachlan, but what if that's because she was purposefully choosing not to, the same way she once had?

She wanted to believe Lachlan, but she didn't want to be played for a fool. Not again.

If it weren't for the house keeping him here, maybe he would've left sooner. It was her fault for thinking he wasn't here just because he was being held here against his will. It was her fault she assumed that he was actually growing to like her company and develop feelings, and not just convenient ones.

It was her fault she allowed him to get so close.

He was planning on leaving. He was always going to leave. Because he never had any real intentions of staying. Lachlan took a slow step toward her, like the floor was ice and at any second, he would hit a thin patch and fall into the freezing pond.

"Eliza." He took another step forward. "I know you've been hurt before. I know you're pushing me away because this between us is all so new and honestly a little terrifying. And yeah, that text from my sister certainly didn't help. But I—" He stopped just shy of touching her, dragging another hand through his hair in frustration.

"I care for you, Eliza. More than I expected to. Embarrassingly, more than I should after less than a week's time. And I don't have any plans on disappearing. You've taken me by complete surprise. You and your wonderful baking, and your brilliant heart. I see a girl who's been hurt and had her heart broken by a prick who wouldn't step up and be the man she needed him to be. But I stayed. I showed up. I helped. I believed in you even when you didn't believe in yourself. That's what it would be like, even outside of here. I wouldn't give you a reason to doubt us. But if you did, Eliza, I'd be here to remind you."

"I'm not asking you to fix me, Lachlan." Her cheeks burned scarlet. A lot of that just sounded like codependency. She didn't need to hop from one relationship to the next. She needed to save herself from getting hurt again. She needed to protect her own heart, not give it away to Lachlan for him to have the power to shatter.

"I'm not trying to fix you. This is me trying to be *there* for you."

She stood, making her way over to the island, needing a second to cool down, to think clearly about what she wanted. What she actually wanted, and not what this stupid week-long retreat made her feel.

If she was being honest with herself, she wanted Lachlan. She wanted a shot at it with him. But things were never as simple as the magic let on.

She looked for Puffcake, missing his comforting warmth on her shoulder. He was nowhere to be seen, except for the tiniest sliver of his tail peeking out from underneath an upside-down mixing bowl. She couldn't help but feel grateful that he was giving them at least a little privacy.

"That's what scares me."

"What scares you?" he asked.

"You say you don't have any plans on leaving, and maybe you don't. Not now, anyways. But what if one day you do? Maybe not next week, or even next year, but a couple from now. What if you realize I'm too complicated, too annoying, too much, or not enough?"

As if on cue, the front door popped open on an invisible flurry of wind. Snowflakes spiraled inside and melted on the warm cottage floor, even though the fire inside the hearth was dying.

A *thump* sounded on the sofa. Eliza looked over to see Lachlan's bag and all of his things zipped up in his luggage. His eyes were wide, seemingly just as surprised as she was.

Because even the house knew. Lachlan wanted to leave. Why else would it be giving him an out?

Eliza looked at him, her eyes glistening. "That was not me," Lachlan's own eyes pleaded with her. They were so big and full, and like molten chocolate. She stared deeply into them. She wanted to believe him. She really did.

But that was the problem.

Even he was too good to be true. Too kind. Too handsome. Too good. Isadora believed she had a good thing until she was left alone with nothing but a note and an abandoned home the very next day.

Maybe Isadora hadn't seen the signs, either, but they were there. But once she finally did, it had been too late. Ernest was already gone.

A happy ending wasn't how this ended for Lachlan and her. The gingerbread house was cursed, after all. Maybe Isadora was right in trying to protect future women from the same fate.

"It's been fun, Lachlan." She breathed at last. "But even the house knows what's for the best."

"Eliza—" He started, but she backed away from him.

"Go." She swallowed back the tears. "Please."

She blinked, and a tear fell. Lachlan blew out a frustrated breath, but he didn't object. Didn't say a word. Just crossed the room to grab his things.

He stopped at the door and turned. One last chance for Eliza to take it all back if she wanted—and she almost did. The words were on the very edge of her lips, ready to slip by.

But he slipped through the door quicker than she could speak. The lock clicked into place; one final note, the ending to some old, sad song.

She heard the engine of his rented Land Rover flare to life, and the house didn't protest as the wheels crunched through the freshly fallen snow and down the long driveway.

The record player scratched to life, the slow drawl of "*I'll be home for Christmas*" piping from the disc.

The magic was still here. But Lachlan was gone.

Chapter Twenty-Two

A Recipe For Goodbye

L ong after the snow had settled from its earlier storm, and the stars had sprinkled themselves across the sky like a topping to a complicated recipe, Eliza did what Eliza did best: she baked. Lachlan truly wasn't coming back.

He'd left at the first opportunity, probably hopped on the first class train to be with his mum and sister for Christmas instead of being here. Or he might've just driven straight home, going ninety to nothing to get out of this crazy town so he could get back to selling his million dollar coastal mansions.

Eliza knew that once they both traveled their separate ways home, and left the gingerbread walls and enchanted kitchen behind, they both would chalk up this entire week to being some odd fluke. A sugar-coated fever dream.

Puffcake tried to console Eliza by wrapping himself around her on her shoulder, nestling his nose into the crux of her neck. She stroked his spine lazily, the tears seeming to come at random.

The house had also tried to console her plenty of times. The kitchen egged her on into using the recipe books in the cabinet, and sugar and butter made their way onto the kitchen island without Eliza even having to pull the ingredients down herself. It knew exactly what she had in mind, except she didn't want to look at a single recipe card.

This time, she wanted to bake straight from memory.

This was her nan's recipe. Which, she supposed, most of them were. At least, the fundamentals were always her nan's. But this one was something her nan was famously known for back in her quiet corner of London: her Victoria sponge.

It was a five-layered cake with a thick homemade buttercream icing between each piece of fluffy vanilla cake, spread with raspberry jam in between. Her nan made it every year for Christmas, but that was about the only time of year she did because it was about as extensive a recipe as one could get.

But that was the point tonight.

If she started now, she might finish before sunrise, but she wasn't in a hurry.

Eliza wrapped her apron around her waist, tied her long blonde strands into a pony, and pulled her last scrap of dignity together. She wouldn't feel sorry for herself. She came here to do exactly this: bake in the best kitchen in all of Britain—possibly all of the world. Lachlan only did her a favor by leaving her alone.

"Guess this is what I wanted from the get-go, isn't it, Puffcake?" she sighed. "Good riddance."

At least that's what she told herself, anyway.

Even Puffcake seemed to see straight through the lie.

They were never meant to last. Their love—if it could even be called that—only lasted a week. She'd known biscuits to have lasted longer before they grew stale.

It was her fault for thinking it could last, her fault for even hoping.

But it was Christmas Eve, and she wouldn't think about him anymore. He was gone, never coming back, and so she would put him behind her, too.

This time, there would be no magic to help her bake. She didn't want it. Didn't need its help. What had the magic of this house really helped her do besides show some memory-preserved recipes, a sad love story, and that love is cursed? She mixed the cake batter without a lick of magic, even hand-poured her own extracts, and opened the drawers on her own.

After about the third or fourth offer from the house, and Eliza's refusal for help, it seemed to get the hint. She wanted to be left alone. Completely.

She just hoped the house wasn't offended enough for the oven to not work.

She placed the first round of cake batter inside, and didn't know she had been holding her breath. She was waiting, staring into the oven for several seconds.

Surely, something else is bound to go wrong tonight, she thought. But it never did.

She absentmindedly pulled the first cake out of the oven when it was done and set it aside to cool before pouring the batter into the pan and repeating the process. Add the ingredients into a bowl, stir, and pour into a pan. Add the ingredients into a bowl, stir, and pour into a pan.

Repeat. Repeat. Repeat.

She didn't want to think. Only wanted to bake a cake ten stories high if she had to. If that's what it took to forget.

Her hands and face were coated with flour and sugar, and for a moment, she could feel his hands brushing hers. The warmth of his laugh, the way they threw heaps of flour at each other, and the warmth in Eliza's chest as he leaned in to kiss her.

And the way he looked at her … It was like she was the only person in the world.

How could that have only been *last night*?

Everything changed in a day. Not even a full twenty-four hours.

Now, nothing would be the same again.

Nope. She wouldn't think of him. Wouldn't allow him space to tear her heart apart again.

She decided to check her phone. When all else failed, some mindless scrolling always did the trick, right? Four texts from Piper, two from mum, and one from Gretel.

> Christmas morning tomorrow at your place? We'd love a round two of the snowball fight if you're down!

Eliza read the message, and read it again, her throat aching. She backed out of the text thread, not emotionally ready to respond to her friend just yet.

She'd failed. The cottage's curse had won. Eliza just wasn't ready to admit it, yet.

She checked the messages from Piper.

> did you build a snowman today and watch it come to life?

> what's next, a reindeer with a glowing nose?

> i just don't understand how you're so lucky.

> HAVE YOU GUYS KISSED YET

So much for some mindless scrolling.

She needed to bake. Thinking would come later.

Eliza resumed building the cake layer by layer, laying the cake and then spreading the cream cheese on thick. The process was almost as mindless as the first portion had been, except she allowed her mind to wander back to her nan. Back to simpler times, when the only worries Eliza had was getting batter on the table because she wasn't quite tall enough to see over the counter.

She embellished the finished cake with vanilla curls, letting them fall onto the top of the finished dessert like snow. Then, she stepped back to admire her work. It was almost too beautiful to eat.

But when Eliza went to take the first bite, she didn't even worry about slicing off a piece. She dug her fork right in, ruining the wondrous work of art, and scooped up the biggest bite she could muster.

Upon taking that first bite, she remembered her nan's giggle, crisp and jovial. Suddenly, it was so sharp in her mind that it brought tears to Eliza's eyes. Not sad ones, as they usually were when she thought of her nan. These were happy ones. Ones that spoke of the years of happiness and wisdom her nan had lived. The legacy she left behind in both love and sugar.

Eliza couldn't help but be grateful for this week away, even if it wasn't how she envisioned it. Even if she was still really sad about how things were left off with Lachlan. She knew the one person who she could talk to.

Her mobile began vibrating on the table. She answered with a sigh, and an excited "*Hello*?" from her best friend came through before she could even put the screen to her ear.

"Hey," Eliza's voice cracked.

There was a beat of silence on the other end of the line. Then, finally Piper's voice again, this time clipped and worried. "Oh no. What happened?"

Eliza guffawed, "Seriously? All I said was 'hey.'"

"You're my best friend," Piper reminded her. "I know your 'hey.' This is a sad 'hey.' So, spill the tea. What's wrong?"

Eliza glanced at the tree. The colored lights blurred together behind fresh tears. She swallowed down what felt like shards of glass, her throat tightening as she managed to say, "He left. For real this time."

The house even helped him pack up his things. The house had known he was ready to go.

Piper sighed heavily. The kind of heavy breath that said everything. "I'm so sorry, Eliza."

"It's okay." She wiped her nose with the back of her hand. "I just feel so stupid."

"You're not stupid. You let someone *in*. Do you know how rare that is for you? What he did says more about him than it does about you."

"It feels like a dream. Like I made it up," she murmured. "Like it never should've happened."

"You didn't make it up. Just because it ended fast doesn't mean it shouldn't have happened. Maybe it was to help you get back out there again and not be so hung up on Davis. Never liked that tosspot, by the by," Piper added in, (as if she hadn't told Eliza before). "Anyways, you were there. He was there. The flying gingerbread dragon, on the other hand, I'm not so sure about ..."

Eliza gave a half-smile. She'd told Piper about Puffcake, but she didn't believe her, even with a picture to prove it. Eliza swore up and down it wasn't AI, but Piper still was unconvinced.

"It just sucks. I was starting to trust him. It felt like maybe it was the start of something good. It felt so different from Davis." Eliza swallowed hard. Her hands shook all over again, and she tossed a hand towel aside in frustration.

"I know," her friend said softly. "You deserve better. You always have."

"Why are you so good at this?"

"Because I've had practice. Remember *the Great and Tragic Banana Bread Incident* our freshman year?"

Eliza laughed despite herself. "First off, I thought we both took an oath to never speak of that ever again. And second, if we *were* going to speak of it, that was different. I set the entire oven on fire in food tech. I wasn't crying over some dumb boy."

"And still, I was there for you. Just like I'm here for you, now," Piper said.

"Thank you," Eliza blinked back a tear.

"Always."

Street lights flared to life and came beaming in

through the kitchen window. But it was almost midnight —the street lamps were already supposed to be aglow. Eliza's heart took a leap in her chest, but she didn't dare pull the curtains back for fear that she wouldn't see what she'd hoped for. Her heart simply couldn't take it. At this point, it might've been more realistic if it were Santa Claus who visited the cottage than Lachlan.

He was already well on his way back home by now.

"Do you think he was going to tell you before he left, if it hadn't been for you confronting him?"

"I don't know," Eliza shrugged. "The house packed up his things in front of me and let him leave, so I'm assuming it knew he was planning on it. Just didn't know how to properly tell me."

Bang!

A car door slammed shut outside. Puffcake snapped his head up from inside his mixing bowl bed.

"*House*?" repeated Piper. "What do you mean the house let him leave?"

Eliza didn't answer right away. She stayed frozen in her spot, mobile still pressed to her ear, heart racing in her chest. Her eyes flicked to the door—still unlocked.

Somewhere in her mind, she'd left it open for him to come back, even though she hadn't truly expected him to. But now, her breath caught.

What if it *wasn't* him? What if it were someone else? A stranger or an actual serial killer this time? The final twist to a very long, very strange holiday.

But would that honestly be more realistic than

Lachlan coming back? And was that seriously where Eliza's standards were, now? Expecting less out of Lachlan than a murderer?

Jingle.

The doorknob turned. Opened.

She couldn't believe her eyes. Dark, brunette hair and her favorite pair of chocolate brown eyes slowly came from around the doorway.

"I gotta go," Eliza whispered.

Piper sputtered. "Is everything okay?"

Click. Eliza ended the call.

He stood just inside the doorway, his cheeks flushed from the cold and his hair tousled from the wind. They both stared at each other. Puffcake sat in the middle, his round eyes darting between the two of them.

Lachlan was *back*.

They opened their mouths at the same time.

"I–"

"I didn't—"

They stopped. An awkward silence stretched between them. The hum of the oven. The crackle of dying embers in the fireplace. The patter of melted snow from Lachlan's coat. It was like the entire house was holding its breath, waiting. Expectant.

Lachlan held out his hand. "You first."

"No," she shook her head. "You."

He shifted his weight and ran a hand through his hair, looking to the floor. "I just wanted you to know that I didn't want to leave."

Eliza furrowed her brows. "But you did leave."

"I know." He blew out a breath. "I'm sorry. I didn't know what to do. I wanted to respect your boundaries when you told me I should leave. I really just wanted to grab you up and kiss you, but when the house packed up my things … I thought that was it. I was sure you truly didn't care to see me ever again. But I had to come back." His voice suddenly sounded like gravel. "I just had to."

"You … *had* to?" she repeated.

He nodded.

"What, did the house forget to pack up a pair of your favorite holiday socks?"

"No." He raked his fingers through his hair again. "I had to see you. Even if it was the last time. Even if you screamed or kicked me out, I knew I had to at least try."

He inched forward, and Eliza didn't move. She stayed rooted to the spot, her heart pounding. Step by step, he slowly closed the space between them. Each step felt like he was closing an impossible distance, like it would stitch back the miles that had grown between them in a span of a day.

Lachlan's hand twitched at his side. He was close enough to touch her, and he looked like he was physically agonized by the restraint.

"I never got to tell you what I wanted for Christmas," he said softly.

"You can't be serious," Eliza muttered.

He gave a small smile, sheepish. Nervous. Sad, yet hopeful. "Ask me," he said.

She crossed her arms and forced her voice to remain level. "What is it that you want?"

His eyes searched hers.

"I want a shot. With you. No questions asked. No anxious thoughts or self-sabotage. No over-thinking. Just … a shot. A real chance." He swallowed hard, "I want you to be my girlfriend."

Eliza just stared at him. The weight of his words settled heavily between them. For a moment, she didn't speak. Her chest rose and fell in uneven breaths, her arms still folded over her heart like armor.

She wanted, more than anything, to fall into him. To give up the fight, to surrender to her feelings regardless of how terrifying they were. But Eliza saw it *all*: laughing and kissing the night of the contest, then she saw the door swinging shut behind him as he departed without a word.

He said it wasn't because he wanted to leave, but that he was respecting her wishes. And granted, *she* had told him to leave …

"I want to believe you, but I'm scared," she admitted. Why did it take *so much* just to speak the truth? It was so much easier to protect herself. To tell him that he needed to leave, even though all she really wanted was for him to stay. She wanted him to stay and fight with her. *For* her.

"I am too." He took a careful step closer. "And I promise, I'll never make you wonder if I walked out that door on my own volition again. This isn't just some holiday fling that I'll forget as soon as I rev up an engine or board a train. I don't just want you for Christmas—I want you every day after, too." His hand rose to her cheek, brushing a stray blonde hair away from her face. His fingers lingered there, his eyes drifting to her lips, then back to her eyes.

At length, Lachlan raised his brows. "So can I have you, Snow?"

She blinked back tears, her heart feeling like it'd been thawed from the fortress of ice she'd incessantly kept frozen up around it since her breakup. Lachlan had swooped in and changed it all, showing her what it was like to have someone actually care. Because even in their best moments, Davis had never fought like this for Eliza. She was always too afraid to speak her mind around him for fear she'd rock the boat too hard and he'd send her overboard.

With Lachlan, she'd had no energy left. She hadn't been searching for love, or anything romantic of the sort. The cottage still brought them together, and she'd been entirely herself. Still, Lachlan chose her. Despite it all; despite the baggage, the failed business, the sappy baking escapade, her closed-off heart.

He'd taken it all. And he still said yes. He still came back.

At last, Eliza nodded. It was such a small gesture that if Lachlan hadn't been searching for it, he might've missed it.

A smile flooded across his face. He leaned in, tentative, searching her eyes for any apprehension. His lips left hers with a gentleness she'd never known before; it caught her off guard. The kiss was soft at first, careful. Like either of them could shatter the moment if they made one wrong move.

It deepened, just a little, and she tilted into him, allowing her guard to drop a little lower.

Eliza turned to the Gingerbread Snap Dragon, still in his usual spot. His gumdrop eyes blinked up at her longingly, silently pleading, '*Please don't forget me.*'

Her heart twisted. She didn't want to leave this place without him. Not after everything.

"What about you, Puffcake?" asked Eliza. "Can I have *you*?"

Puffcake's eyes grew incredibly round; it looked like he was giving her his equivalent of the puppy-dog stare. Then, he gave a joyful snort as he wagged his tail so fast it knocked over the jar of coconut flakes.

Eliza laughed through the lump that had formed in her throat. "I'll take that as a yes."

He bounced to his paws, his biscuit limbs shaking with excitement, already eager to follow her to the ends of the earth—or at least out the front door.

Then, Eliza returned her attention back to Lachlan.

"You sure you want this?" She raised her brows. "The sentient gingerbread and my weird baking obsession?"

"Especially those things." Lachlan smiled down at her, his voice unwavering.

They kissed again, this time warmer and deeper than before. Sweet like honey, and everything she'd been too afraid to say out loud to him until now. Because things between them were just a *maybe* or an impossibly hopeful dream.

It was a yes.

She couldn't possibly know for certain that they were endgame, but she hoped with all her heart. And that was a start.

She allowed herself to fully melt into his embrace, wrapping her arms around his neck. Puffcake gave an excited screech before blowing smoke in the shape of a heart. He fluttered his tiny icing wings over to the hearth and settled himself there, his back turned away from them to give them privacy.

Before she knew it, Lachlan was grabbing her by the back of her knees and lifting her up onto the kitchen island. His hands came up, tangling in her hair, pulling ever-so-slightly to tilt her head toward the ceiling.

He attacked her in a series of swift kisses all along her cheeks, forehead, chin, and nose. Eliza erupted into a fit of laughter, her heart feeling like it might burst right out of her chest from the pressure.

The old grandfather clock struck midnight.

Ding, dong. Ding, dong. Ding, dong. Twelve times. It was Christmas.

When they finally pulled apart, Eliza was breathless. She rested her forehead against his, unable to stop grinning like a madman.

Lachlan placed the gentlest of kisses on her forehead and whispered, "Merry Christmas, Snow."

Chapter Twenty-Three

The Master Sweet

The cottage had bloomed with magic, color, and vibrant, twinkling lights. Best of all, piped icing floated down from the rafters, the green mistletoe responding to their reunion.

The curse was gone. Eliza had felt it.

Slam!

Isadora's Memory-Baking Cookbook flung itself from the cabinet and onto the floor. The sound startled Puffcake into flight, his icing wings flitting at a hundred miles per hour. He rolled his eyes when he saw it was just the enchanted cookbook wreaking havoc again before settling himself back down on the windowsill. Puffcake shot Eliza a pointed glare to communicate, *"Really? This bloody book, again?"*

Eliza laughed and rustled Puffcake's chin. "Lighten up. I'd be a grinch too if my husband left me during

Christmas." She bent down to retrieve the book, but noticed something peculiar. With furrowed brows, she thumbed through the pages. The recipes she'd baked from earlier in the week were still there, all of them Isadora's … but this time, at the back of the book, there were new recipes. These were Eliza's.

She blushed when she even read *Eliza's Award-Winning Winter Hearth Scones* had made the cut, but the last recipe brought tears to her eyes. "*Marjorie's Christmas Eve Snowflake Cake*"

This was the recipe she'd made on Christmas Eve after Lachlan left. She'd bet anything that if she were to make them as the book instructed, she'd see herself standing with her arms crossed, worry painting her face as Lachlan tried to assure her that the text from his sister wasn't what it looked like. She'd be willing to bet that the vision would be of her standing in the kitchen, alone —much like Isadora was all those years ago.

She was also willing to bet the vision would show Lachlan coming back.

Because her story didn't have to end like Isadora's. Lachlan was willing to stay, and not for some fun, Christmas fling. He came back. He never even wanted to leave in the first place, but it had been Eliza who pushed him away out of fear.

She'd rewritten the history of this cottage. She and Lachlan had broken the curse, and this cookbook was evidence that the magic still existed. (Apart from the abnormally bright lights coming from the Christmas tree, the self-playing record, and the sentient ginger-bread Snap Dragon on her shoulder.)

"What is it, Snow?" Lachlan yawned as he came up from behind her. He grabbed both of her hands in his and swayed them to the rhythm of the carol playing on the record player.

"It's Isadora's cookbook, the one you tried baking in. Look, it even wrote down your recipe."

There it was: *Lachlan and Puffcake Pancakes: Best made the morning of Christmas Eve.*

Lachlan chuckled. "I'm flattered to have made the cut. Were they really that good?"

"No," Eliza answered truthfully. "But apparently, Isadora thought so. Or maybe it was just the thought that counted."

"Probably that," he said, leaning in and kissing her softly on the cheek. "Permission to say that the kitchen is your domain from now on?"

Eliza smiled. "Permission granted. But I'll leave the barbecuing up to you in the summertime. I'm a lousy griller."

"I can handle that. As long as I get to wear the apron you think I look sexy in."

"Get your own!" Eliza batted his hand away as if he were trying to steal it from her now. "Gretel gave me this one!"

"Fine." He swung Eliza around, and pulled her tightly into his chest. He looked at her with so much longing in his eyes that it made her weak—and Puffcake annoyed. He flapped away to the living room to give the two of them privacy.

Roaring filled their ears, and something like the sound of biscuit crumbs breaking apart filled the entire cottage. Lachlan furrowed his brows, looking out the window to see if another blizzard had struck. Eliza followed his gaze to find the snow falling in a lazy mist.

The floor rumbled beneath them as the snapping sound still reverberated through the very structure of the cottage. Pictures on the wall shook, the glass bottles clinked together on the shelf, and the copper pots swayed overhead. Flour particles drifted through the air like settling dust.

What was going on?

Then, the rumbling stopped. The house settled. If it hadn't been for the looks of bewilderment on both Lachlan and Puffcake's faces, Eliza would've wondered if she'd imagined it.

Then, Eliza saw it, down the hall. The cottage had *expanded* on its own. Another suite opened up that hadn't been there before.

For a moment, the three of them just gaped, unable to speak.

Eliza could make out the golden bedframe, baked to perfection, with a patchwork quilt and several matching pillows. The sight made her blush.

"Did the house just create a master bedroom?" Eliza asked.

"I think so," Lachlan said. "I guess so we both have

a place to stay when we come back here." Then he smiled.

Eliza looked up at him, hopeful. "You really would like to come back here?"

Lachlan nodded. "Of course. Every Christmas. I'm not lying when I told you this has been my favorite Christmas yet. It even tops the year I got an Xbox 360. And that was a good year. Didn't come out of my room until Easter."

Eliza laughed, then turned her attention to Puffcake. "Has the house ever done this before?"

Puffcake shook his head violently.

Interesting. So the cottage not only no longer held a curse that broke up entire marriages and relationships, but it now answered to Eliza and Lachlan's love.

Love. Who was she kidding?

She'd known Lachlan for six days. But she knew his past, knew how he took his coffee in the mornings, how he strictly took long showers. She knew that his favorite color was orange, and that his favorite dessert was cheesecake (which she thought was dreadfully boring). Although he had said that her fondant fancies might've changed his mind.

She'd come to know so much about Lachlan in such a short amount of time. Sure, there was still so much more to learn, but wasn't that the wonder of loving? To keep knowing? To keep growing?

It wasn't the house that broke up marriages—it was the couples themselves. The cottage only ignited the problems that were already there, and when times became too hard, they'd give up. It was the *people*—not the circumstance. Because Lachlan and Eliza had been together far less time, and they still found a reason to fight for what they had.

Lachlan turned to her. "I don't know why it made us a separate bedroom. I liked the couch just fine. And I don't think Puffcake was running out of space on his side of the bed upstairs."

Puffcake gave a look that said, "*Speak for yourself.*"

Eliza laughed. "I certainly was. Who knew a kitten-sized pastry would take up so much space?"

"Beats me." Lachlan smiled. "Wanna go check out the master suite?"

Chapter Twenty-Four

Christmas Day

Lachlan, Eliza, and Puffcake followed the breadcrumb trail back up to the Gingerbread Hollow Square. And, as before, Puffcake would stop every few paces or so to eat the timeless treats.

Lachlan laughed at the sight. "You know, I wondered this last time. Is this considered cannibalism for Puffcake to eat bread?"

"Only when there's cinnamon involved," Eliza answered.

"Which is like, fifty percent of all baking dishes," Lachlan pointed out.

"So? You drink black coffee," Eliza shot back. "You

wouldn't know sweetness if it hit you in the face with a whisk."

Puffcake gave a dignified huff in agreement. Once they were at the market, Eliza insisted that they separate in order for her to find him a present.

Lachlan decided to take Puffcake, the two of them smiling together like they were in on some sort of elaborate plan, but Eliza didn't push for details. She only agreed to meet them both back at the cottage in an hour.

In the market, she found a new mug and a pair of Christmas socks for Lachlan. For Puffcake, she bought a tiny, doll-sized scarf and a pair of matching mittens for his paws. (She had to ask the clerk for an extra pair of mittens, since he has four paws.) She even found something for Hansel, Gretel, and Piper while she was there.

While she was heading home, the nostalgic smell of chocolate wafted her way, and she realized it was Frank's chocolate shoppe, Mendel's Confections. She hurried into the shoppe, the bell above giving a jingle. Frank looked up from behind the counter, his grin warm and friendly. The display case before her sparkled with colorful éclairs, fondant fancies dusted in gold, and— Eliza's heart leaped.

There were gingerbread snap dragons. She recognized the swirl of pink and blue icing wings, the sprinkle of coarse sugar of the dainty nose, complete with lavender gumdrop eyes. She *knew* these creations. These were *Isadora's*.

Of course. Frank was practically ancient. Perhaps he knew Isadora personally.

"Mr. Mendel?" Eliza called his name a little louder than necessary. She felt silly, but Frank inclined his good ear to her, furrowing his bushy, white brows.

"Is there something I can help you with, young lady?"

"Yes," she said. She wasn't sure how to ask. "Do you know where these recipes came from?"

Frank's eyes lit up, the blue sparkling with excitement. He didn't say anything else, but pointed out of the window and to the lamppost directly outside the chocolate shop. She headed outside of the gingerbread-trimmed door and found a plaque on the lamppost.

In Loving Memory of Isadora and Henri Mendel Founders of Mendel's Confectioner's Shoppe, Est. 1966, whose love story began in chocolate and lives on in every sweet creation. Their son, Frank Mendel, carries on their legacy with the same passion for artistry and heart that built this haven.

Eliza took a step back. Frank hadn't just known Isadora—he was her *son*.

A slow grin crept across her face. Isadora had not only found love, but she'd built a life with someone who shared her passion for baking. She'd fallen for a chocolatier, and together, they'd had a son.

She wondered why Isadora never lifted the curse

from the cottage on Drury Lane. Perhaps the memories of her first marriage were too heavy to face, and so she never returned to it. Perhaps she even tried to undo it, but didn't know how.

Either way, Eliza couldn't help but feel overjoyed. Finally, there was closure.

Getting a spark of resolve, Eliza stepped back inside and approached the counter. She pulled *Isadora's Memory Baking Cookbook* out of her satchel and placed it on the counter in front of Frank. "I believe this belongs to you," Eliza said. "Your mother would want you to have it. She loved you more than you could ever imagine."

Frank looked at the worn cover and then up to Eliza. Tears shimmered in his deep blue eyes, and for a split second, Eliza swore she was staring into Isadora's. Suddenly, everything fit.

That's when she saw the black and white photograph on the wall: the two shop founders, so happy and full of life. Isadora stood next to her husband, with one hand cradling her round belly and gleaming with a very large ring on her finger.

Guess Mendel's Confectioner's Shoppe paid well, Eliza thought, smiling.

Beside her, Henri gazed down at Isadora. He was tall and handsome, with dark hair and a strong jawline. He looked like a much younger version of Frank. He paid no mind to the camera, but only stared at Isadora, like she hung the stars and moon themselves.

"Thank you," Frank said. "Please, take whatever you'd like from the shoppe."

Eliza just smiled. "Actually, now that you mention it, I'd like to ask a favor. Would you mind if I used your recipe for Gingerbread Snap Dragons in my own bakery back home in London?"

After all, she knew the recipe by heart.

Lachlan and Puffcake were already outside by the time she arrived, her arms full of all the wrapped presents.

Opening the door, Lachlan took them from her, and placed them inside. When she tried to help, he was adamant that she remain outside. He moved away from the door, and Eliza caught a glimpse of a wreath hanging there.

That was odd.

That wasn't there before.

Lachlan came back outside, shutting the door behind him. "Before we go inside, I wanted to give you your present first. You ready?" he asked, brows lifted.

Eliza nodded.

He came over to her, grabbed her shoulders, and spun her around three times. The snow crunched beneath her boots and threatened to make her slip, but with the help of Lachlan steadying her, she stayed upright.

At last, he stopped her in the very same spot she'd been standing in before. The cottage was as it was before, sugar-laced piping on the roof, candy cane lights leading up to the front door, smoke billowing from the chimney.

The only thing different was the wreath. She looked at Lachlan, confused. He was holding a set of keys. "Well?" he jingled the keys. "What do you think?"

She blinked, looking between Lachlan and the set of spare keys. Surely, they were the spares. They couldn't be …

"I bought it," Lachlan filled her in.

Her hands flew to her mouth as she let out a screech. "What? *How*?" That was all she could get out.

Lachlan smiled. "For you. I was surprised when I saw the Sugar Plum Suites owner was in yesterday, but then again, it is holiday week, and it's their busiest month out of the year. I went in and ended up making him the offer. It's completely in your name, Snow. You can Airbnb it out and make a profit for your bakery, or you could move in here and grace Gingerbread Hollow with your baking all year-round. The only thing I ask is that every Christmas, this is where we'll be. Together."

Together. He'd said. *Every Christmas*.

And he was nowhere on the lease. He had no intention of screwing her over by ever trying to take this beloved place from her. She looked at the cottage. *Hers*.

She fell into his arms, tears streaming down her face as she kissed him. He hit a patch of ice, and the two of them went tumbling. The fluffy snow broke their landing, and she fell onto his chest in a flurry of giggles.

She kissed him again with every ounce of love and joy she could possibly convey to him. She felt like the Grinch; her heart only expanded more and more every time Lachlan was around.

"Thank you," she whispered. Her lip quivered, and Lachlan kissed her back delicately. The way he held her face was like he was holding a glass ornament, precious and worthy of being cherished.

"That isn't all," Lachlan mutters.

"What isn't?" Eliza asked.

"Puffcake and I wanted to do something else for you, but thought for this next gift, you might want to be more involved."

"What do you mean?"

"I mean, in the new year, I'll come up and help you search for places in London for your bakery."

"But I—" Eliza stuttered. "—I only have five thousand pounds. That isn't enough to—"

Lachlan cut her off. "Your five thousand pounds has been matched."

"*What*? You can't just do that! I got you a bloody mug for Christmas, and you buy me a house *and* a bakery?"

Lachlan laughed. "One, you just spoiled my

Christmas present. How dare you? And two, I'm not the one who helped match your bakery funds."

"What?" Eliza blinked. "Then … who was it?"

Puffcake came fluttering over, then, eyes aglow with the joy of Christmas morning. He wagged his tail feverishly, snuggling into Eliza.

"*Puffcake*?" Eliza gaped in disbelief.

"Turns out, the exchange rate on chocolate chip cryptocurrency is through the roof right now. Guess that's what living for seventy-five years will get you with nothing to blow your money on but candy cane lattes and frosting facials."

"Guess you could say our gingerbread pal is rolling in dough," Eliza giggled, scratching in between his ears.

Puffcake barked out a laugh, too, and smoke dissipated in the winter air.

"How could I ever repay you?" she asked them both.

"Just repay us in pastries. Word on the street is that the exchange rate for *your* delicious treats is pretty high, so you'll have paid me back in no time."

She kissed him again, and Puffcake flew out from her scarf and bounced wildly on her head. "Puffcake!" she giggled. "Lay off!"

"Jealous, much?" Lachlan said.

Puffcake still pounded away, pointing behind them. It was too late.

A snowball came barreling through the air, smashing both Eliza and Lachlan in the face. A triumphant *"whoop!"* came from the street, and they both turned to see Hansel and Gretel slapping in a high five.

"Nice work, bro!" Gretel's voice glittered through the air.

Eliza shot to her feet, and lent a hand to Lachlan. The two of them smiled mischievously, thinking the exact same thing. Together, they began packing as much snow as they could, hiding behind Lachlan's car.

"You guys are burnt toast!"

Epilogue

Pipe Dream

One year later

"*Three, two, one!*" The crowd cheered from behind Eliza.

She tightened her grip around a dramatically over-sized pair of red scissors, the plastic handles comically bright against her flour-coated hands. Lachlan's fingers settled over hers, his presence constantly grounding her to the spot as several camera shutters clattered in short bursts.

"Ready?" Piper called to them over her phone, her eyebrows raised expectantly as she held her camera high. She was live on her TikTok, smiling into the camera as the hearts were already bubbling up the side of the screen. She stood shoulder-to-shoulder with Hansel and Gretel, trying to coach them on how to "get the best angle." Eliza's parents were beside them, her dad grinning wide, and her mum wringing her hands the way she always did when she was fighting back tears.

On the other side, Lachlan's mum and sister were leaning in so close that Eliza thought they might topple over any second. They were all in the front row, eyes up front, and cameras set. Every face on the street was turned toward them, as their little corner of London seemed to hold its breath for the grand opening.

Eliza took a deep breath and looked to the ribbon pulled taut against the double doors of her new bakery, Puffcake's Pantry. On her shoulder, Puffcake balanced there like a crowned mascot, beaming between her and Lachlan, his chest puffed tall in his moment of fame.

The crimson ribbon fell away, and soon the inside of Eliza's bakery was swarming with customers. It smelled of sugar, and frosting, and—best of all—Christmas.

By the register, several families gawked and pointed at the Gingerbread Snap Dragons lying on trays inside the glass container by the register. With Puffcake's permission, Eliza had thought they were the perfect extra touch to her bakery's selection.

She'd even made tiny little copies of the recipe from back at the cottage. She bent down next to a little girl, her eyes wide with marvel as Eliza handed her the recipe card. A little bag of glitter was tied to the recipe card. "Here, take your dragon, and when you get home, sprinkle just a little bit of pixie dust on him. Then you'll have your very own Puffcake!"

The little girl jumped up and down, looking at her mother, eager to put the theory to the test.

Over in the corner, Eliza could see Lachlan trying to wrap up his visit with Piper, but she'd dragged him in on her TikTok live, talking about the bakery's opening.

He made eye contact with Eliza and silently brought his hand across his throat in a slicing motion, but Piper didn't notice because she was too busy rattling on and on about the shoppe.

Eliza just laughed, watching their interaction play out. They'd met as soon as Lachlan and Eliza had come home from their Christmas escapade. For New Year's Eve, Lachlan had driven up to meet everyone.

He was extremely nervous, but as soon as they were around him, he meshed so well with them the way he did with everyone he met; it was like he'd known Piper and Eliza's mum for years.

When he finally was able to break free from Piper, he made his way over to where Eliza was standing in front of the entrance of the bakery.

She breathed in the faintest hint of evergreen, and she was taken back to another time, another place. Where the two of them met, where the two of them fell in love. She'd never forget, but it was nice to be reminded of such a sweet time in her life. "I just love you," she sighed on the exhale.

"Yeah?" Lachlan's upper lip twitched, "I just love you too."

"Thank you," she whispered. The back of her throat burned. She bit the inside of her cheek, forbidding herself from crying, but it was too late. The tears swelled in her eyes and blocked her precious view of Lachlan.

"For what, Snow?" His voice was low and tight, brows knitted together in concern.

"For proving me wrong. For sticking around."

A smile broke from his lips when he realized her tears weren't sad ones, but happy ones. He bit his lip, and looked to Puffcake, who was resting lazily behind Eliza.

"About that ... there's something we've been meaning to ask you."

Before Eliza could ask, Lachlan was bending down on one knee. The ring was suddenly there, the box open, the diamond sparkling like stars behind a backdrop of night. Eliza's mouth dropped open in surprise.

"I promise to stick around like the black nasty snow in winter. Puffcake also gives you his word, too, but I told him that he couldn't piggyback off of me. So ..."

Puffcake came fluttering over, and in his claws was a picture of the gingerbread house, the three of them together in front of it. And when she looked close enough, a white speck of something like flour coated her blonde hair and rosy cheeks.

"Is that ...?"

"Flour." Lachlan nodded. "So you'll never forget where it all began. And that every year, we'll go back to right where we started. To *our* cottage, to our annual flour fight—"

"My answer is yes." Her voice came like a whisper, but in her heart, she'd never felt more certain about anything in her entire life.

Lachlan rose from his crouch and scooped her up, twirling her around and around. He kissed her endlessly, and it felt like an oven had swelled to the hottest degree in her chest. It wasn't an uncomfortable heat, but only the kind of warmth love and pastries could bring.

It all felt like a pipe dream. Puffcake quite literally was—baked with real gingerbread and piped icing. Lachlan, on the other hand, was just a lucky, once-in-a-lifetime find. For an entire year, she kept waiting for the high to crash, for her fondness to spiral, or for his to wane, but it never did. Their love only grew sweeter as the days stretched on.

Lachlan slipped on a patch of ice that sent the two of them tumbling to the ground in a heap of laughter and kisses. His coat and the snow broke their fall.

"Just so you know, I'll win the flour fight every time," he grinned up at her. Lachlan pulled her to him, cupping his gloved hands between her cheeks. She couldn't help but smile as they kissed. Slowly, she moved one of her hands to gather snow and splatted it on his face.

"I think we should let Puffcake be the judge of that."

Acknowledgements

Grandma, this book was inspired by you. You taught me how to cook, bake, and to believe in the magic of Christmas. As a little girl, I thought the magic came from Santa, all the lights and presents under the tree, and those silly little festive earrings you'd always wear. But now that I'm grown, I realize the magic all along was simply being with you. I'll keep your traditions alive through my stories and talk about you often to your grandson. (He would've loved you, by the way.)

Granny, I love you and all the wonderful years we've been blessed to spend together. I hope you *loved* the flour fight scene! That memory of us throwing flour at each other in your kitchen has stuck with me all these years, and I'll always treasure it forever.

To my husband, the one and only book boyfriend inspiration I'll ever need! You, my love, are endlessly sweet, forgiving, and kind. Thank you for being my constant source of love and encouragement.

Mom, for *always*—and I mean always—believing in me. For cheering me on and showing me how to be a good mama. For teaching me the magic of Christmas and the most important meaning behind it.

To my precious baby boy, I hope I can make every season of life a magical one for you. Mommy loves you so much.

Ashlyn, thank you for your friendship, support, and laughter through every journey! You make my life so much brighter.

Ioana, for taking this manuscript and getting it where it needs to be! You're amazing. I am endlessly grateful for your sharp eye, patience, and dedication to making my words shine. I look forward to your red ink marking up many more manuscripts to come!

My readers over in Florence's Fables, your encouragement and support have meant the absolute world to me. Thank you for joining this adventure, and for helping me bring my stories to life.

A HUGE thank you to Stephanie Hooper, for being my British dictionary! Your list of suggestions was incredible. Thank you so much for your attention to detail and generosity in helping me revise my manuscript so it feels that much more authentic.

My lovely future readers, thank you for stepping into Gingerbread Hollow with me. I hope it feels like home.

Finally, to God, for giving me the gift and opportunity to do what I love.

About the Author

Florence Gray writes magical love stories with far more color than her name suggests. She's a full-time artist and a full-*full*-time mom, and somehow landed a man patient enough to handle anything—even her. You'll usually find her wrapped in a blanket cocoon between diaper detonations, too many iced coffee refills, or battling a futile war against the dog-hair tumbleweeds from her two German Shepherds.

For more books and updates:

www.florencegray.org

instagram.com/morallygrayauthor
tiktok.com/@Letstokbooks
goodreads.com/Florencegray

More sweet things are
happening in Gingerbread
Hollow...

Boo, Again

Coming October 2026

Also by Florence Gray

Tales from Gingerbread Hollow

Boo, Again (Forthcoming)

The Crystal Seas Series

A Sea of Blood and Sapphire

The Cloak and Dagger Duology

The Heartbeat Heist

The Power Play (Forthcoming)

Standalones

The Popstar Playbook (Forthcoming)